ACK TWEEDALE STREET
A YORKSHIRE CHILDHOOD
RICHARD ALEXANDER

WORKBOOK PRESS LLC
187 E Warm Springs Rd,
Suite B285, Las Vegas, NV 89119, USA

Website: https://workbookpress.com/
Hotline: 1-888-818-4856
Email: admin@workbookpress.com

Ordering Information:
Quantity sales. Special discounts are available on quantity purchases by corporations, associations, and others. For details, contact the publisher at the address above.

Library of Congress Control Number:
ISBN-13:   000-0-000000-00-0 (Paperback Version)
                000-0-000000-00-0 (Digital Version)

REV. DATE: 29/04/2022

Contents

This book is dedicated
to the memory of my
Father,

Richard

Thanks for your care, the fun we had in
childhood and the chats over a beer or
two in a manhood. Unfinished, sorely
missed and never forgotten.

The Awakening

When was your first recollection of being very much alive and on earth? can you remember it as vividly and in as much detail as I? No one remembers the experience of birth or indeed being a baby but when awareness sets in then life becomes a reality. I suppose this happened to me around the age of four during the Christmas of 1951. The festive seasoned should always be a time of happy memories and this year certainly was despite post war poverty and rationing. There was a feeling of optimism in the air that things could only get better.

Tweedale Street was a peculiarity of the North of England and consisted of a long grimy terrace of stone houses built "back to back" each house having a front door only. One side of the terrace fronted the street without the benefit of a garden while the other side faced a cobbled yard, dustbins and the outside toilet block. Facing the street was regarded as the upmarket portion of the terrace but passersby on the pavement could look directly in through the windows. Our house faced the scruffy old yard where all the washing was hung out to dry but at least it was close to the outside toilet block which was handy on the dark and rainy nights.

Originally built by mill owners to house their workers in Victorian times the houses were still rented out to working people and contained an interesting cross section of northern working class life. Most occupants were relatively poor mill and tannery workers who tended to work in close proximity to their housing. Most walked to work, some rode bicycles, a few had motorcycles and none had cars. Residents of Tweedale Street tended to fall into two distinct camps, the clean working class, although poor, had great pride and would be spotless with neatly patched somewhat threadbare but clean clothing. Their houses would be spotlessly clean even if the furniture was second hand and had seen better days. In those days very few women, particularly those with young families, went out to work and the respective roles of husband and wife were very clearly, if somewhat rigidly, defined. Competition in terms of cleanliness between neighboring housewives was very fierce and this was evidenced externally by the whitening of the stone entrance steps on a daily basis. Wo betide any man in a dirty job who came home and disturbed this domestic perfection particularly if he stepped on the newly whitened threshold. Having overcome this obstacle, it was wise to call for newspapers to put over the clean flagged floor to allow him to remove his dirty outer garments and leave them on the newspaper for washing. His meal would always be waiting for him as would the tin bath by the fire if his occupation was in the seriously dirty category, the class leader by a considerable distance being the miner or coalman who could arrive home so black as to be hardly recognizable.

These decent hardworking people had often not had the opportunity of a good education or had little ambition in themselves being resigned to follow the well-trodden path from school to mill. However, many had much higher hopes for their children to escape the mill through the gateway of education via the local Grammar Schools.

At the other end of the sliding scale were the dirty working class who often lived in the same areas but were governed by a totally different set of values. Many came from inadequate and broken homes and some from parents who had lived in the same way and were now perpetuating the species. Descendants of immigrant labourers and tinkers and gypsies who had decided to settle down were represented. This group was characterized by the "breadwinner" usually being permanently out of work and supported by welfare payments bolstered by a large and ever increasing brood of children, nine or ten being quite usual. This happy go lucky attitude and work shy existence was often passed down from generation to generation as the children found it impossible with such a home background to break out of the mould.

The dirty working class tended to spend very little time working or attending domestic chores. Apart from the weekly trip into town to sign on and collect the dole money most of the time was spent lounging on the sofa, visiting the betting shop and frequenting the pub. Some practitioners raised the stakes of slothfulness to new heights by ordering a taxi for their trip to the dole office one and a half miles away rather than walking or taking the bus. In an age before wide availability of television entertainment was somewhat limited and these families would often have a new child every year to add to the chaotic domestic squalor and at the same time improve the level of welfare payments. Children of these families were allowed to roam free from a very early age with- out supervision and it is a miracle that so many of them survived to adulthood.

To qualify as really poor on the Tweedale Street sliding scale a family simply had to have more than one dog. A couple of large and somewhat vicious Alsatians would ensure serious street credibility otherwise two or three flea ridden mongrels would complement the eight or nine flea ridden children to add to the squalor and general chaos. It was not unusual to see dog dirt on the floor with crawling babies picking it up and handling it inquisitively. Privacy was at a premium and the only means of bathing was by filling the tin bath by hand which demanded so much effort many lazy people would not bathe for months on end. Body odour was therefore rife and some personal hygiene problems would present the most optimistic deodorant manufacturer with the challenge of a lifetime. Houses stank abominably of the stale food, particularly cabbage. Such was sloth in some households that dirty plates and rubbish were left on tables adding to the smells. A woman may have three children still in nappies at any one time and if washing had not caught up with demand they were allowed to roam free to urinate and defecate wherever they could. Dogs were allowed to run wild and often had pups who for some reason would find the security of the inside of a sofa appealing and would make their home in it popping out through holes in the fabric much to the surprise of visitors who were about to sit down.!

The real nightmare for all the clean mothers was her children mixing with the dirty children and catching head lice thus passing them on to the rest of the family. Once every two weeks at school we had to endure the attentions of a lady affectionately known as "Nitty Nora the lady explorer" as the nit nurse was known. We would be called individually to the front of the class and made to stand on sheets of white paper while Nora combed our hair vigorously and often painfully with a special and very fine toothed comb.

The rest of the class would lean forward on their seats in anticipation gazing intently at the paper and enjoying your discomfort and embarrassment.

They were looking for the tell-tale little black dots jumping around on the paper which would signify a successful comb.

If any nits were spotted the poor victim would hang his head in shame particularly if he came from a clean family and he could then look forward to the anti-nit treatment which was vigorous washing of hair in a strong and foul smelling shampoo designed to kill them.

The poor victim could look forward to playground taunts for weeks to come and a degree of social banishment in the short term.

Houses in Tweedale Street were very basic with two bedrooms on the first floor with neither plumbing nor heating. On the ground floor was one room which served as lounge dining room and kitchen combined. This room had a sink in the corner and an open coal fire which was the only means of heating the house. In the cellar below there was a meat safe with a grill front designed to keep meat cool and mice out prior to the availability of refrigeration. The cellar was also home to a family of mice who always seemed to thrive despite the regular use of traps. Privacy in such a small house was minimal and even clean families only used the tin bath once a week as it had to be filled and emptied laboriously by hand on each occasion. Ill-fitting sash windows did little to keep the house warm and frost and ice could form on the inside of the glass overnight. The toilet was a shared arrangement across the yard with no heating or lighting, pieces of newspaper for toilet paper and a collection of the biggest spiders ever seen. The toilet was particular fun on very cold days when both cistern and pan froze solid, it was best avoided completely at night as it was impossible to see the spiders.

The back yard was paved with cobbles with tar between them. In the summer sun the tar became flexible and could be prized out of the joints by use of a stick and used for play in a similar way to plasticize. Unfortunately, it was a dirty shade of black and left stains on hands and clothing much to mother's horror and disgust.

The immediate environment outside the yard was what could best be described in planning parlance as one of "mixed uses". Small corner shops and pubs supported local residents and a variety of industry was mixed in with the predominantly residential area. In those days the "living horizon" was only as far as you could venture in a day by walking, cycling or by bus, perhaps ten miles. Families were only likely to travel further on the annual holiday which may entail a train journey of eighty miles to the coast by train.

In the vicinity of Tweedale Street was an assortment of industry which would be regarded as the equivalent of a Russian Environmental disaster today. Tanneries adjacent to housing gave forth with the most disgusting smells and used an enchanting cocktail of lethal chemicals which poisoned both air and land. Hides hung out to dry dripped chemical pollutants onto the ground and stank like something out of hell. Asbestos and chemical industries added to the cocktail a little further afield, but the undoubted king of the locality were textile and Woollen mills. These mills produced cloth for much of the world using robust machinery designed and built in the Victorian era. Many mills specialized in the recycling of Woollen waste known as "shoddy" which gave off its own distinctive and unique smell difficult to compare with anything else known to man. The majority of men and some of the women living in the vicinity worked in this industry. When I was a little older and allowed to roam around the area we used to look into the mills and factories and gaze in awe at the noise, dust, wheels turning, belts driving and workers using sign language to communicate because of the noise.

However, the greatest opportunity for childhood exploration was undoubtedly the slaughterhouse a couple of streets away. The building had a small yard surrounded by a high wall which it was possible to surmount with some difficulty and sit on the top to see what was going on. The view was like a vision of hell with blood running in the gutters, intestines being coiled up like clothes lines and sad looking cow's heads staring out from hooks and shelves. The view made me feel quite sick initially but I quickly became used to it and the men would waive cheerily as our heads appeared over the parapet.

Although I had a brief acquaintance with mill work in my youth, unlike many I escaped a lifetime of repetitive work by using my brain and pursuing other avenues which opened to me.

Mischief and Play

Today we seem to have accepted the fact that our little darlings have lost the use of their legs and must therefore be ferried everywhere. This applies even on short journeys and preferably in four-wheel drive monstrosities more at home in the African bush. Increasing traffic levels and crime may have something to do with this but the child develops with poor traffic and street awareness to say nothing of a poor physique.

One of the joys of reaching the tender age of seven was the complete freedom to roam far and wide usually in a small group. The long summer holidays with mild weather and light nights was the best time for this. We saw many things which would be just a blur from a passing car and there was always sufficient of interest to keep us occupied all day. They were lot of potential hazards and dangers contend with but surprisingly few mishaps.

On the opposite side of the valley to our house and about one mile away was an enormous rubbish tip which served the entire town and surrounding areas. This monstrosity was crawled over by giant diggers and lorries looking like matchbox toys while massed regiments of seagulls wheeled and screamed above searching for food eighty miles from the sea. To reach the tip we had to cross a road then traverse a terrace of scruffy run down shops with steel shuttered windows, next was a railway line and once safely across we stood just three fields away from our objective. The fields were full of half wild and distinctly unfriendly long haired gypsy horses enjoying a bit of free grazing and we gave these a wide berth particularly as their owners could be around. The final obstacle was an evil smelling and distinctly polluted black water stream full of discarded rubbish such as old prams, bedsteads and oil drums. The thought of falling into this horrible black soup defied imagination but thankfully there were a couple of makeshift timber bridges across it.

Most of the time we visited the tip to search for items to play with and undoubtedly the best day for this was Monday when a weekends tipping remained undisturbed. On a good day a veritable treasure trove of discarded junk could be found. Particularly prized were discarded prams which could be made into trolleys, old tyres which could be rolled along with the aid of a stick and any old bikes which could be cannibalized for parts to keep your own going. The possibilities for play were endless, we made dens from materials found on the tip and floated other items down the stream on lengths of string. We found old radios and dismantled them for their components, the valves being particularly prized.

Other kids could be quite tough in this environment and there were many who had an even more basic upbringing than I. One friend of mine was proudly returning home one day with a particularly nice tyre when he was stopped by another lad who had taken a liking to it and offered to fight him for it. My friend agreed and they wrestled and grappled with each other all over the dusty path finally ending up in a ditch. Unfortunately, the challenger proved the stronger of the two and my friend had to part with the tyre with a resigned shrug and a handshake. Rough justice maybe but both accepted this as a normal convention with no outward sign of emotion.

From time to time gypsies would camp on this land seeking to make a living from scrap from the tip, the odd bit of casual work and a considerable amount of petty thieving. Pilfering activities were aided and abetted by the womenfolk who would go round houses in the vicinity selling wooden clothes pegs, the odd lucky charm and tea towels. Most housewives would buy something, no matter how small, to avoid the gypsy curse which the women were supposed to invoke and bring down on anyone who refused to buy. On the sales trips the gypsy women would gain valuable intelligence on insecure and unoccupied property which often helped then men in undertaking a little creative burglary in the evenings. Any property undergoing renovation by the council was fair game and anything portable and saleable would be stripped out in no time and sold for scrap. When things got too hot with police interest or local resentment the gypsies would normally just move on. What most people resented about gypsies was that they were rarely seen working, paid no taxes, but nevertheless had a good standard of living with fancy chrome bedecked caravans and often expensive cars or pickups. We always gave these people a wide berth as they owned fearsome dogs who would go mad if you approached the camp. They would alert the camp by barking even if you were hundreds of yards away. Gypsies were very much a law unto themselves and on a sliding scale of roughness were close to the pinnacle. Their children were brought up to run wild from birth and were often illiterate and never attended school. They used the fields as a toilet and quickly developed skills such as kicking the half wild dogs if they stepped out of line.

If the summer weather was good, there were lots of opportunity for further adventure and exploration particularly around old or abandoned buildings. One large sinister old house in the vicinity was set in its own heavily wooded grounds and contained a small orchard. Most of the local kids were too frightened to venture into it as it was reputed to be haunted and certainly felt spooky. The owner was a little old lady who was wizened old crone and reputed to be a witch with special powers. However, the orchard was particularly tempting as it contained fat sweet and succulent eating apples which were the best in the district. Allowing ourselves half an hour to talk ourselves into it and gain some false courage we approached the house, scaled the boundary wall and peered over the top. So far so good, no sign of the old crone or anyone else. We dropped over the far side of the wall and crouched in the undergrowth looking and listening intently for any signs of life but all was still quite. However, the hairs were standing up on the back of my neck and I still felt uncomfortable as I had a feeling someone was watching me. We crept through the undergrowth towards the orchard and as I approached the best tree my heart was pounding as I was sure I could hear a dog in the grounds. I stayed motionless for more than a minute but there was no sight or sound of life. The best tree was a little more difficult to climb than I had anticipated but I made it and began to pick the forbidden fruits and stuff then in my pockets. My descent from the tree was somewhat quicker and I ran out of that evil and spooky place as fast as I could still have convinced I was being watched by some malevolent force. Once over the wall and clear of the scene of the crime my heart stopped racing and my thoughts turned to the contents of my pockets. I pulled the best apple out of my pocket, polished it on my jacket sleeve, and bit into it vigorously, no apple has ever tasted as good!

Another favourite spot for a summer visit was "seckers" pond which never dried out in the summer and was seriously deep in the middle. Local folklore said it was bottomless but I believe there was an old mine shaft in the middle which flooded when abandoned. Regardless of the truth this all added to the sense of mystery and danger surrounding the pond and increased the fear factor among young explorers. Most lads were happy enough to swim or paddle around the edges but no one was brave enough to swim across it for fear of being sucked down by some strange force. I always thought lads were in greater danger from getting cut by or tangled up in all the rubbish in the pond rather than being sucked down in the middle but I still wasn't brave enough to swim across. The pond was a great place to spend a sunny afternoon looking for frogs and newts, fishing for sticklebacks with nets, catching small roach and perch with rod and line and generally getting exceedingly dirty and muddy. There was also the added attraction of fishing out old junk that others had thrown in to see if it was useful or not.

When we ventured further afield we would often cross town and visit Calms wood but this had to be done with some care as we were in hostile "enemy" territory where there were lots of lads and other gangs unfamiliar to us. Calms wood wasn't a wood at all but a steep grass covered hill part of which had been quarried in the past. Its main claim to fame was that it was the only place in town to have been bombed by the Germans in the Second World War. Folklore tells us that the Germans were really aiming for the Sheffield steel works some 30 miles to the south and were somewhat off course. The real truth may be that a bomber got lost and decided to jettison its deadly cargo on the nearest town before heading home. Generally, the Germans were not interested in bombing the Woollen industry but Sheffield with its massive steel industry was a prime target. The wood was known as a favourite quiet spot for courting couples so the German activity that night may have made the earth move for more than one. The resulting bomb craters formed magnificent play areas with a degree of authenticity for military style games bearing in mind their origin. Some of the craters filled with water but dried out in the summer when we would all search for bomb fragments or anything hidden by winter water.

The river Calder meandered through the town but was rather less than pretty as it picked up polluted water from more and more industrial outflows on its journey to the sea. I often thought that by the time it reached journeys end it must be nearly solid with the effluent picked up on route. The river was a marvellous area for adventure and exploration though it was dangerous, often fast flowing and heavily polluted. It claimed a couple of lives a year, sometimes children but also adults many of whom could not swim in those days. People who fell in but survived seemed to pick up all sorts of ailments and infections from the dirty water. Such was the pollution from the textile and other industries that no fish could survive and the only life in the river were large and rather nasty looking water rats. At weirs or bends in the river the chemical pollutants in the water would create massive amounts of foam, the tops of which would blow away in windy weather and create visual spectaculars on adjacent roads and streets. The exploration challenge on the river was to find items of junk discarded by the river on slow bends and retrieve them by climbing down the bank or grappling them with hook or line. The ultimate challenge which I started but did not finish involved crossing the river on a huge metal pipe belonging to an adjacent mill. The pipe had a system of handgrips on top to allow secure fixings for painters and maintenance men but nonetheless it was a heart stopping journey across the pipe looking down at the black fast flowing stinking river. Unfortunately, if you were dared to cross you had to take up the challenge or lose face, the secret was to go but go slowly. By proceeding very slowly and carefully you did not fall off and stood a good chance of being spotted by the mill workers who would shout at you and tell you to come back. This is exactly what happened when I attempted it, so honour satisfied, I made my way back.

It was really quite surprising just how close the open countryside was in those days but the difficulty was getting to it as few people had cars, a minority had motorbikes and the majority used public transport. Pollution thankfully tended to diminish as the distance from industry increased and fresh air could be combined with exercise even if the setting was only a bleak exposed moor above your mill town. One of my favourite visits to the countryside was to visit dear old Mrs. Spencer an old family friend who lived on and ran a smallholding outside York. After the grimy cobbled streets of home never far from the noise of industry the sheer space, peace and quiet of the countryside was a revelation. We could run wild around the farmyard, through the barns and out into the fields in complete freedom. We made dens in the adjacent woods and barns, climbed trees, went fishing with nets and jam jars in ponds and streams, absolute bliss! However, my favourite pastime was finding and collecting the eggs from the barns. Hens are crafty creatures and they continually find new places to nest where hopefully they and their eggs will remain undisturbed until incubation has taken place. It was terrific to go on an egg hunt every morning armed only with native cunning and a small bucket. Most mornings I would find between six and twelve eggs. My reward on return was a pair of soft boiled eggs from the ones I had gathered together with fresh bread and butter, who could wish for more.

When the winter snow descends upon the dark land it is always time for play. Forget the biting wind and cold, find the sledge in the cellar, polish the runners and go for it. Sledges came in a variety of guises from sleek shop bought tubular steel models to all sorts of homemade contraptions with varying levels of sophistication. Living in a relatively hilly area there were lots of opportunities for high speed runs but unfortunately very few of these devices had any brakes. The ideal location therefore was a downhill stretch leading to an uphill stretch to slow the sledges down naturally. Lots of people would frequent the best slopes giving lots of opportunity for snowball fights among rival gangs and for the older boys to try to push snow down the jumper of their favourite girl. Returning home wet and cold but jubilant after an afternoons sledging was simply wonderful particularly if a hot drink awaited to warm the hands and stomach. The innocent play of childhood can still get you into plenty of trouble. One afternoon I was in the house playing on my old wooden rocking horse when I thought I would play a game around a real horse and cowboy galloping as fast as they can to escape pursuing Indians. I stood up on the rocking horse pushing it further and faster than ever before. The frame was starting to lift from the floor and I passed the point of no return and crashed onto the floor head first over the horse, taking the horse with me. Unfortunately, the horses head had pierced the radio which was my parent's sole source of musical entertainment in the days before television. Just as well I was too young to understand the feeling of guilt!

I wasn't very popular after the rocking horse episode but managed to make myself even less popular a few days later. Dad had decided to redecorate the living room, he stripped off the old paper and started to hang the new. Having finished papering one wall he decided to have a break before trimming the top and bottom of the paper. I thought this an opportune time to make amends for my rocking horse episode and decided to give him a hand. I located the trimming knife and started to trim the paper at the bottom. Unfortunately, I cut the bottom three inches off to an irregular pattern leaving the final edge one inch short of the skirting board so my poor old long suffering dad had to start all over again.

My younger brother Ron was very naughty and he had a particular habit of annoying girls, particularly our cousins when they came to visit. Together we would dream up all sorts of pranks to keep them on their toes. One of his favourites was to slip his pet mouse into the cousin's doll and pram usually under the doll. He then hid to watch the result knowing that by the time she reached the end of the yard the inquisitive mouse would have popped out and dear cousin would be running up the yard screaming while we would all falling about speechless with laughter.

Occasionally a female cousin would come to stay and she was rather bossy and self-opinionated and in turn this would drive us to play a prank on her. When she was out we would enter her room and secure some fine, almost invisible, fishing line to the foot of a chair by her bedside passing the line under the rug and out of the door leaving the end tucked under the landing carpet. That evening we would casually mention that we thought the house was haunted and we had been frightened by strange movements of objects in the cellar. Mother dismissed the idea as did bossy cousin and eventually we all retired to bed. Ron and I gave her 15 minutes to settle down and then crept quietly out of our room and located the end of the fishing line on the landing. A slow and careful tug made the chair move slightly and we knew she had noticed it as she moved in the bed. A few minutes later we gave a hearty tug and the chair moved about a foot from her bedside and across the room at which point cousin let out an almighty scream and Ron and I dashed for our beds and pretended to be fast asleep. Mum came up and calmed dear cousin down saying it must have been a nightmare or something but she didn't find the fishing line which we removed at the first opportunity the next day. She looked in on us but we were fast asleep in our innocence and therefore she didn't suspect us and had nobody to blame. Dear cousin was badly shaken and didn't sleep too well that night thinking of our haunted house!

Pets

The dark winter nights had set in and the snows had done their worst covering the landscape in a blanket two feet thick which smothered all noise and hid all but the taller features. From the relative warmth of the house I looked out onto that grey winters afternoon where all was still and the whole world appeared to be sleeping under the cold white blanket that had fallen the night before.

To the front of the house the road was devoid of traffic, most vehicles and drivers having given up the unequal struggle against the elements and vehicles stood inert at strange angles awaiting the normality which would return with the thaw.Groups of excited children had claimed the road for themselves and were sledging along shouting and tumbling in the deep snow, making snowballs with cupped hands, throwing them at friends and then rubbing and blowing on hands to restore circulation.

Restless with being indoors I decided to wrap up warm and venture out to explore a nearby area which was a peculiar piece of wasteland covered with scrub and trees. Some of the trees had been felled but left in situ to be eventually swallowed up by the undergrowth thus forming part covered dens in which we often used to play.

I trudged across the barren landscape silent and still when suddenly the slightest of movements caught my eye. At first I thought it was my imagination but as I peered further into the gloom I could just make out a black shape moving slightly against the background of snow. It had moved into the far end of one of the dens below the fallen trees and looked like a small animal. I wriggled into the den and then remained motionless for a few minutes straining my eyes to make out what the creature was. There it was again a black shape moving in the snow. I fixed my eyes on it and crawled slowly up the den towards it. As I got closer I could see it was a large bird with the distinctive black and white plumage of the magpie. I gently reached out for him and after a token resistance involving much flapping of wings I picked him up and carefully tucked him inside my coat to keep him warm. I hadn't realized in my excitement just how big magpies were and clearly he was exhausted and significantly weakened by the severe weather. Excited by my unusual find I raced home through the snow to show it off to my parents and younger brother. Bursting in through the door I pulled the magpie out of my coat rather like a magician pulls a rabbit out of a hat. A fully grown magpie is a large bird at close quarters andthe whole family admired my unusual find. First of all, I had to find a box for him to make him feel secure and then position him near the fire to keep him warm. I then gave him some bread and milk but he didn't seem to be particularly hungry. Over the next couple of days, he settled in quite well and became used to my approach. I had hoped he would recover from his exhaustion so that I could release him back into the wild but sadly he died on the third day. I really missed my beautiful bird with his inky black plumage and snow white breast. I buried him in a special place near the den where I found him once the thaw had set in.

One of my uncles used to breed cocker spaniel dogs as hobby and on my eighth birthday he presented me with a beautiful jet black puppy. Unfortunately, he forgot to consult my parents first so the gift caused some consternation particularly for my house proud mother. We had never had a dog in the house before and mother, who kept a spotless home, quite rightly considered animals and cleanliness to be incompatible. He was a lovely little dog with a shiny black coat and inquisitive playful nature of a puppy which made him so endearing to children. I was very proud of "Jet" and bought him a collar and lead. I used to take him for walks around the block so that all the Neighbours could admire and make a fuss of him. However, Jet had one major problem which revealed itself when we retired for the night. He was so used to sleeping with his mother and the rest of the litter that being left downstairs alone he became unhappy and insecure and let everyone know by howling continuously. This went on for several nights and the only remedy was for him to sleep in my room on a blanket but mother would not hear of this as she was terrified that we would be infested with dog fleas. After a week of sleep deprivation and a standoff with mother something had to give and unfortunately this had to be Jet. It was with a heavy heart that I was obliged to give him back to my uncle who I know felt sorry for me and said that I could come and take his dogs for a walk anytime. I cried every night for the next few nights as I really missed Jet but armed with the resilience and tenacity of youth a couple of weeks later Jet was just a distant if pleasant memory and I had my eye on a couple of ferrets which horrified my mother even more.

Christmas Treats, High Days and Holidays

With few luxuries available on a day to day basis Christmas was always a time to look forward to.Items appeared in the shops that were simply not available at any other time such as bananas, oranges, dates, nuts and selection boxes full of chocolate.We looked upon these items with great anticipation and as real treat but these are merely commonplace today as living standards have improved.In the absence of television which had only just started to become available at great expense people actually visited and talked to each other or played cards and board games which were very competitive and great fun. Radio was also extremely popular and of surprisingly good quality particularly the plays and music programmes.Holidays were less generous than today with most people enjoying a couple of days for Christmas and a couple of weeks in the summer when the mills closed down.

Christmas was defined far more by the spiritual element and much less by materialism in those days. Even if money was available goods were often not and the system of rationing limited the amount of non-essential items such as sweets via the mechanism of coupons. The ultimate childhood fantasy was an entire Mars bar particularly as the rationing system allowed only one per week and this was usually cut into slices to be shared or savoured at a slice per day. My first recalled Christmas did however involve a small taste of the technology to come when Dad borrowed a new style portable wind up record player from a workmate. These were the new and much smaller versions of the bulkier wind up models with the big horns which have now become collector's items. Unfortunately, due to the rationing system records were in short supply so the modern marvel only had three singles to play in mono through its tinny little speaker. By the end of Christmas, I knew them all off by heart but the one that lodged in my mind forever was a somewhat banal but catchy little ditty called "Animal crackers in my soup"!

One of the main customs over the festive season was visiting and being visited by friends and relatives. In those days it was very unusual to work away from family roots unless serving in the military and it was almost unknown to work in the next town or county. Skills were not as readily transportable, for instance, a weaver in the mill could only find employment in Yorkshire or Lancashire. Business had not yet developed the global reach or footloose capability they have now. The travel horizon for a young family with children in tow was no more than five miles on a bus but this would usually be sufficient to cover the majority of relatives and friends. Relatives were a somewhat diverse bunch with widely different habits and customs. They were mostly employed in Woollen mills, tanneries and the chemical industry and lived in council housing as home ownership among working people was virtually unknown. Lack of television and other sophisticated forms of entertainment encouraged visiting and it gave us children a wider range of potential playmates.

A few characters among the relatives really stand out the first being dear old aunty Hetty who was tall, thin as a rake, gruff of voice but with the appetite of a lumberjack. She could eat more than any other person I had met and when she visited us and attacked the cold buffet you could guarantee a table at the end of her stay that looked as if it had been visited by locusts.

Uncle Conray was another character, he was Polish and had married into the family after the war. Rumour had it that he had a rather murky past in the Polish resistance involving night time operations against the Germans. He operated on an unlit motorcycle across country and while often heard was never detected. Having successfully evaded capture he lived to work the rest of his days in the safer but less exciting grimy mills of Yorkshire. Even after many years in England his accent was still thick and impenetrable and he had some very strange ways. At a time when many people led a precarious life often running out of food and money before pay day at the end of the week Conray was an exception. To venture into his cellar was rather like visiting Aladdin's cave with neat shelves stacked high with the most amazing selection of tinned food I had ever seen and certainly enough to survive a major disaster. When asked why he kept so much food Conray became a little withdrawn and somewhat reticent but I found out later from my aunt that it was something to do with nearly starving to death during those dark and desperate days with the resistance.I would love to get him to open up and talk about it for there must be an incredible story to tell but so far I have been unsuccessful.

Uncle William was the only member of my family who could remotely be considered as middle class.He was the only one who could be sent to Grammar school, the traditional route upwards for young people, and the family had to make great financial sacrifices to even make this possible.Visits to his house were always a revelation but often a trial for us kids unused as we were to tablecloths, fine China and side plates.I am sure mother used to be terrified we would break something but thankfully we usually managed to keep things intact.Uncle William was a navigator in the RAF during the war involved in risky flights over Germany in Mosquitos, a fast fighter bomber constructed mostly of timber and fabric. He was shot down over Germany and spent the latter part of the war in a prisoner of war camp.He was another who never spoke about his experiences until recently when he started to open up a little.

My uncle Alvin was a strange character somewhat abrupt and taciturn he nevertheless had a heart of gold.In his youth he had been a keen cyclist and when he found out about my interest in the sport he asked me if I would like an old bike in his shed.When I said, yes please, he opened the door of his dark and cluttered shed and wheeled out a dusty and rusty old racing bike.The wheels and Tyres were long gone but the frame was a rare lightweight Saxon model with twin down tubes.I was so excited as I knew I could rebuild and repaint it into the bike of my dreams. One year later I finished it just about the time I was actually tall enough to ride it.My first journey was to take it back to Uncle Alvin to show him the finished product and he was very impressed.I thanked providence that Alvin had four daughters and no sons otherwise the bike may never have come my way. Over the next few teenage years the bike was to give me great personal freedom and pleasure.

One advantage of regular relative visiting was to compare different modes of transport.Boys would compare trolleys and bikes while the men would compare motorbikes.The trolley or soapbox was a very versatile piece of transport all homemade and varying in build quality and sophistication. The best examples were greatly admired by other boys and at times like this you wished your father was a carpenter.Basic construction was two pairs of recycled pram wheels, a good solid wooden chassis, primitive lever rear wheel braking and a steering system consisting of a large nut and bolt holding a timber cross member steered by the feet.Normally these contraptions would carry two people but were also useful for raising pocket money by carrying heavy objects for old people and those without transport.Over the years mine carried bags of coal, furniture, rabbit hutches and an assortment 0f other items. Trolleys were also useful for taking girls on the back and impressing them with the downhill speed as the trolley was as close to the ground as a modern go kart and the impression of speed greater than the reality.

Transport for most people in those days meant buses with the odd train journey around the annual holidays.For most the aspiration to car ownership was still light years away but many men had motorcycles particularly to get to work and back.My father and his friends and relatives had all sorts of machines at different stages in their lives.The most popular commuter bike was the ubiquitous BSA Bantam, often ex GPO, bought for a bargain price and offering robust simplicity and reliability if not much excitement.Other machines were a mixture of BSA's, Velocettes, Aerial, Royal Enfield, Douglas, Norton and Vincent.Unfortunately, a few years down the line nearly all these famous names would go out of business after the impact of the Japanese motorcycle invasion which offered greater reliability and sophistication.Another popular means of transport was the motorbike and sidecar which is now almost extinct.A young blade could have a powerful 650 cc bike when single and still retain it linked up to a sidecar when life caught up with him and marriage and children came along.Sidecar chassis were normally bought off the shelf and bolted on to the motorcycle frame.Sidecars could be bought but many owners built their own to suit their particular needs out of timber sheet steel and aluminum. By the standards of today and with a build not dissimilar to a caravan they were decidedly unsafe, however I can recall very few accidents involving them probably because they were almost exclusively family transport and sidecar attachments made it impossible to corner fast.

What the motorbike and sidecar did provide were many happy family holidays and day trips to the fresh air of the seaside away from the grimy industrial towns.However, it could not provide for all transport need as I recall when we moved house.Dad, a small but immensely powerful man moved all our modest possessions two miles to our new home using nothing but a hand cart.Although we had relatively few possessions this still involved several large wardrobes and two tons of coal as a grand finale.

Pollution and other Entertainment

The magic of the seaside with its fresh air, bright and brash attractions and atmosphere of fun was in stark contrast to the grey and grimy reality facing our trippers when they returned home. Within a two-mile radius of my home I could count no less than twenty-three mill chimneys all spewing out smoke and pollution. Just in case this wasn't enough there was back up in the form of five cooling towers and emissions from other industries such as tanneries and an assortment of metal bashers. This was one of the few parts of the country where women hung out the washing to get dry and dirty at the same time. However there were worse places to live, my uncle was a miner in the aptly named Grimethorpe not far from Barnsley which was definitely top of the pollution tree. I always thought during family visits to Grime Thorpe that the town had been created to make most other places on earth look better hence visitors would leave in good spirits. It certainly worked for me and I could never understand how my uncle could work all day in the dirt and dust of the pit and then return to the surface and enjoy a different kind of dirt and dust.

The impact of all this pollution was devastating in the long term on everything and everybody.A walk around the local cemetery on a bright sunny day would show a host of graves of people who died in their forties and fifties, long before their normal lifespan should have ended.My town was known as the heart attack capital of the country assisted considerably by poor diet, excessive fat and heavy smoking. The impact on buildings was just as bad, fine stone and brick would go black over the years, compounding the dark and gloomy nature of towns and cities.Acid rain would soak brick and stone corroding surfaces and causing them to crumble away. Privet hedges were a dirty grey in colour and on a wet day the dirt could be wiped off the leaves to reveal the original green below.

The massive pollution also created the most awful fogs and smogs which would linger for days asa damp oppressive blanket coating everything it touched and swirling round in varying intensity.It was easy to imagine shapes and objects approaching through the mists which would turn out to be mere illusions.

A trip into town on the local bus is one of my most vivid memories and as an antidote I started dreaming of the sort of sunny island paradise depicted in the Bounty chocolate bar advertisements as an escape from the awful reality.I approached the bus stop through an almost impenetrable drizzly smog to find eight other bundles of humanity already in the queue but unrecognizable as they hunched down into their coats to escape the elements.Some were sniffling and fighting off winter colds, others had sticking plaster on their necks hiding weeping and suppurating boils which were so common in those days as a consequence of poor diet and pollution. The whole queue looked grey and miserable as they shuffled around to keep warm and shrank into their coats to escape the elements.

The headlights of the approaching bus made a feeble effort to pierce the morning gloom and the crowd shuffled forward in anticipation of some warmth and shelter. Most of the men sought a seat on the upper deck where smoking was allowed and they climbed the stairs with much coughing, wheezing and clearing of throats. I climbed the stairs to the upper deck and was greeted by a scene akin to entering Dantes inferno with great clouds of acrid smoke billowing around and low visibility courtesy of rudimentary lighting. Smoking in those days was considered manly for some obscure reason and an adult male nonsmoker in a manual occupation would be regarded as an odd ball and somehow not a real man. Women who smoked were often looked down upon and considered rather tarty although the trend for more women to smoke was already apparent.

Meanwhile back on the upper deck our heroes are now on their third or fourth unfiltered woodbine of the day prior to arrival at work where they will spend the day in a polluted atmosphere. A chorus of coughing and clearing of flemy throats announced their arrival, no wonder so many didn't make it past forty-five or fifty as the gravestones in the cemetery bore witness to. Filter cigarettes were considered effeminate, only purchased by women and homosexuals. Real men smoked Captain full strength with the tough bearded sailor on the front of the packet or if money was tight, cheaper, smaller woodbines.

The typical diet in a Northern mill town would have given your average Californian a heart attack as he gazed on in total disbelief.Fish and chips were part of the staple diet consisting of fish in batter and chips all deep fried in beef dripping and saturated with fat.Chips with everything was the order of the day while a typical snack may be bread covered in beef dripping or black pudding which was dried pigs blood with lumps of fat in it.One of the few healthy options was tripe and onions which my father enjoyed but I found revolting as it was basically raw cow's stomach and intestines.

Work had many dangers at this time, young women would work in the mill on weaving looms enduring tremendous noise, breathing in air laden with fibers and communicating in sign language.Many went deaf in later life. Men were regularly exposed to deadly asbestos through pipe lagging, brake linings and building materials.The minute fibres remain dormant within the lungs for years then suddenly become cancerous and active enough to kill within months. Strong men would become old and weak in the space of weeks. Men who worked with dyestuffs in the mills would develop bladder cancers and miners exposed to fine coal dust developed lung diseases.Sadly, in many cases these illnesses would occur towards the end of working life and cut short a well-deserved retirement particularly as many men had a reluctance to visit the doctor until they were really ill.

Entertainment for the majority of people usually consisted of radio, visiting friends, the pub or working men's clubs. Younger people preferred coffee bars which were just becoming popular, the Saturday night dance or the back seats of the cinema where a little privacy with the girl of your choice could be achieved.

For children the three big events of the year were Christmas for presents, Easter for new clothes probably the only set you would get all year and which we usually messed up and got into trouble for. Finally, a week or two at the seaside in the summer months if money permitted. The summer months also gave one or two travelling attractions such as the circus with its pair of old moth eaten elephants and a few scraggy lions. To a child it all looked rather glamorous and exotic if you didn't look too far behind the facade. The second travelling attraction was the

Fair with bright lights, loud music and exciting rides. This was also the place for food with a difference, such treats as candy floss, toffee apples and hotdogs overflowing with onions which somehow contrived to smell much better than they tasted. There were lots of games stalls demanding different skills and giving prizes to lucky winners in the shape of soft toys, coconuts and the particularly prized single goldfish looking lonely and confused in its own little bowl. A visit to the fair was a great opportunity to stay up late even if accompanied by parents as fairs attracted a considerable number of roughnecks and lowlifes. Fairs travelled around a pre-ordained circuit from town to town over the summer months and were usually manned by illiterate gypsy types known as "Feasties". Impressionable young girls would often befriend these characters impressed with their romantic sounding travelling lifestyles. The Feasties themselves had had lots of practice at befriending girls all over the North of England and were adept at attracting sympathy by looking, tattooed, earringed, scruffy and somewhat undernourished. Rather like Sailors they had a habit of having a girl in every town. Unfortunately, some of the impressionable young girls were left with a little more than they bargained for when the fair moved on, often necessitated a very embarrassing visit to the doctor. Worst still it could lead to a significant change in lifestyle about nine months later. Trying to track feasties down for parental responsibilities or medical tracing was almost impossible because when things got too hot on one circuit they would transfer to another.

Undoubtedly my favourite event of the year was the 5th of November or Guy Fawkes plot to blow up the Houses of Parliament. This celebrates a plot to blow up Parliament in the 16th century. On the cold and misty nights leading up to it we used to have great adventures including commando style raids on other gangs of kids using bangers for explosives and occasional jumping jacks to keep the opposition on their toes. This was followed by a stealthy and silent retreat into the night before we could be identified or located.Fireworks had all sorts of experimental and exotic uses in the days before the politically correct nanny state had any say in the matter. Many men were excellent sources of information having been demolition experts or involved in blowing things up in a big way during the war and were glad to pass some of their skills on. One creative routine was to light a banger and then place an old tin can over it to see how high it would be propelled, thirty feet or so was realistic. One other experiment which we undertook, in the worse possible taste, was to place several bangers into a dead cat, stand well back and see what happened.

Possibly the best aspect of the 5th was the bonfire itself. We would collect wood, old furniture and anything combustible in the weeks before or if we couldn't find enough we would appropriate other peoples in the dead of night.After the fire was lit the burning of the Guy as an effigy of Guy Fawkes took place, fireworks were then let off while the fire burned down. Once the fire had died down to a warm rosy glow it was time for all sorts of cooking experiments to take place. Baking potatoes could just be thrown into the fire but the secret was to remember where you had placed them or they would be lost for good.Flour and water mixtures forming a kind of dough could be cooked on the end of a stick and made a passable imitation of burnt bread. The women would prepare mouthwatering dishes of their own including Parkin, a delicious ginger cake, a warming soup of ham scraps and split peas and mince pies hot from the oven. Boys would amuse themselves with lengths of touchy band, a slow burning string for lightning fireworks, and liquor ice stick which was rather like chewing on a flavoured twig.

I suppose the worst time of year was midwinter in snow and freezing conditions despite the attractions of snow for play.When it was below zero we certainly knew it as the only heating in the house was coal fire in the living room and it was always difficult to get out of bed for school when there was ice on the inside of the window pane. Things did not improve when I ventured across the yard to the outside toilet and found both pan and cistern frozen solid.However, the three mile walk to school in deep snow was a marvellous adventure and the perfect excuse for being late particularly as the snow level was above your wellington boots and the journey was across a park where confused ducks were attempting to land on a frozen lake.

School Days and Religion

I suppose everyone remembers their first day at school for better or worse, usually for worse. The strange and unexpected separation from mother, the strange new children you haven't encountered before and a variety of teachers you meet for the first time.My introduction was probably more traumatic than most as the school had the added complication of being a religious one. It was of Roman Catholic persuasion with many of the teachers being nuns and was populated with some rather rough kids mostly from large Irish families who had a tendency to gang together and bully the rest.

The school itself was a rather grim and forbidding dirty old stone building sandwiched between a main road to the front and a railway line to the rear.Adjacent to the school was a vacant site where houses had once stood, on the other side a foul smelling mill dealing with the recycling of "shoddy". The teacher nuns looked rather sinister in their flowing black habits while some of the civilian teachers looked rather oddball too. The playground was all concrete without even a blade of grass showing through the cracks.It was surrounded by a high fence to stop balls straying onto the railway line but that did not stop the adventurous from exploring nearby derelict houses or placing halfpennies on the line to see if the train would squash it to the size of a penny.

Corporal punishment was an accepted part of school life and often given for minor transgressions just as it was by fathers of most of the children who misbehaved in the home. School masters often used a leather belt to keep order but with rough and rowdy children who were regularly beaten at home a certain degree of immunity crept in greatly reducing the deterrent effect.I sometimes felt sorry for the teachers who, despite their natural tendency to lord it over the children, must have faced an impossible task in trying to teach a class of forty rowdy lads anything.Often classes would descend into total anarchy or a comedy show and nothing would be learned. Classes may well have been entertaining but attendance was a complete waste of time.It was obvious to me that many of the kids had no desire to learn anything and were destined to become "factory fodder" in similar way to their parents.This tradition is not just confined to urban living; in the countryside it is known as the "tractor driver" syndrome.

Nuns are strange creatures, many were of Irish descent and few could be described as having God's blessing in terms of looks. Many got the calling when beyond normal marriageable age with a considerable amount of encouragement from their families who in a very traditional society were otherwise at a loss to know what to do with them. A few were soft and angelic born to serve God in chastity and obedience for the rest of their lives. Others were bitter and frustrated by the lousy hand life had dealt them. Living without male company in a room akin to a prison cell is not a natural state for most women and in Nuns, just as in others, it brought out frustration which was released through sadism.Some of them just loved to be cruel and inflicted punishments which were way over the top but were never challenged for their behaviour as they were all perceived to be holy women and the brides of Christ. One of the most feared Nuns punishments was to hit you on the hand with the edge of a 3 foot ruler with sufficient force to create nasty red and purple raised swollen stripes across the hand which were painful for days. It was probably a minor miracle that no bones were ever broken, as far as we knew, by this form of punishment but it must have been a near thing.I am sure my parents must have noticed these bruises but in their eyes the Catholic church and nuns in particular could do no wrong, after all the pope is seen in Catholic eyes as infallible.

There is one distinct advantage in being born on the wrong side of the tracks, so to speak, the only way forward is up! Having been quite a good scholar at the junior school despite all the chaos and even coming top of the class once, much to my surprise, I managed to pass the eleven plus exams which found me in a Grammar school, Roman Catholic of course. This was an event which made both myself and my parents very proud but it did entail a fairly lengthy bus journey to Huddersfield and back every day.A new Grammar school had been set up in a large old house in its own grounds. It was run by the Rosminians, a Roman Catholic order of priests supported by assorted nuns and a few civilians.What they thought of us I do not know for sure but the majority of them had previously taught at a leading Roman Catholic public fee paying school where pupils had well off parents and were supposed to be impeccably behaved young gentlemen.I always took this with a large pinch of salt as these boys' only boarding schools often had drug and behaviour problems plus an undercurrent of homosexuality. Our mixed school was populated with the less well-off and I am sure we were regarded as one step up the evolution chain from savages.

The upside of my new school was that education was good and the setting of the lovely old house in its own grounds was pleasing and conducive to achievement. There were some interesting places to explore in the grounds, hidden greenhouses, overgrown vegetation hiding a summerhouse and secret cellars under the main house.The school was mixed but as eleven-year-old boys none of us recognized the existence of girls in case it was perceived as a sign of weakness by the peer group. A typically modern and much larger school was being built a mile up the road but it would never have the character and charm of the old school.Sunny days were an absolute delight in the old school and we often had lessons and leisure time in the open air.Unfortunately, lunch was typical school dinners of the heated and imported variety supplied via the lowest tender and often quite disgusting in quality. I remember once biting into what I thought was a boiled potato only to find it was a large ball of fat.It never ceased to amaze me that many of the thinnest people often ate huge amounts of food and still stayed thin while fatties often ate less and were much more picky but still remained fat.

One of the priest/teachers was a keen photographer and thanks to him I have an excellent record of my schooldays as he used to wander around the grounds at lunchtime taking photographs which he could later process and pin on the notice board so that pupils could purchase if they wished.

The Roman Catholic Church played a prominent role in our lives, mother being devout and father a little less so. The local catholic school, church and convent were within a few hundred yards of each other and many nuns also taught at the school.

As I grew up and became more aware a lot of things used to puzzle me about the church, for instance poor people were expected to contribute to the collection during a service and yet the church had enormous assets all over the world which rarely appeared to be realized. Could God really condemn a poor soul to eternal damnation merely for missing church on Sunday, surely he is depicted as more merciful. Why should a Nuns love of God bar her from the love of a man and procreation..?

Looking critically at the church it seemed to fit into an earlier age when villages and small towns were dominated by the Squire and the Clergy. All power and influence were concentrated in these two bodies while ordinary people gave a portion of their labours to the squire and the church in turn so that they could live off the fat of the land with very little

effort on their part. At school, particularly in history and religious education I used to take great delight in pointing out the failures of some earlier popes who after all are supposed to be infallible together with similar failings among leading clergy. None of this information was available from school text books but it certainly was from the reference library. Here are a few examples, clergy who bought their positions, Popes who had a string of children often courtesy of nuns and bishops who lived in splendid palaces while their parishioners starved.If God came on earth again I wonder who he would cast out of the temple or perhaps he would appear to be so radical that the authorities would arrest him as a dangerous revolutionary.

The church tended, given its history, to dominate its disciples and rule by fear, promising hell and damnation for a wide variety of misdemeanors. The threat of eternal residence in hell or the statement that children could not enter heaven unless baptized was usually enough to ensure compliance. Often the only remedy to cure the problem and wipe the slate clean, particularly of the more serious hell qualifying mortal sins, was to attend that uniquely catholic institution known as confession. This entails entering an ornate wooden box in a quiet corner of the church where a priest is seated in the other half of the box. Communication is through an obscure metal grill designed to hide the features but allow voice transfer so that in theory at least the priest cannot identify the confessor. The confessor then tells the priest all his sins and often some of his innermost secrets and is then absolved from his sins with a suitable penance usually involving saying a number of prayers a number of times. Thus saved from eternal damnation our hero can then go off and commit a few more sins and the priest, who can probably identify the confessor, finds out what is going on in his parish.

Many of the parishioners were of Irish descent and therefore had this effortless ability to interchange church with the pub across the road at the drop of a hat. The trick was to arrive just a little late and stand at the back of the church thereby ensuring that during a long and tedious sermon by visiting clergy keen to impress, a discrete exit for fortifying refreshment could be achieved. A return for the consecration, which determines attendance, could be arranged and in this way a man's thirst could be satisfied promptly without incurring eternal damnation. On Christmas eve midnight mass was a popular service with drinkers who had commenced the former activity around the six pm opening time. As closing time was around eleven thirty pm this was just about right to make midnight mass and stand at the rear of the church swaying slightly. The drink did loosen inhibitions and allow for joining in the singing with great gusto. The pope was regarded as being infallible but became increasingly out of touch with his parishioners particularly on the subject of birth control which many people used but was regarded as a mortal sin. However, the availability of easy confession soon resolved the problem with a relatively painless absolution.Despite all this the creaking and aged pronouncements from distant Rome were still revered regardless of how out of touch they were and formed the basis of many a long and incredibly boring sermon. The worship of the Virgin Mary was particularly strong and almost a cult among the women.

Unfortunately teaching and sermons tended to encourage pity and non-understanding of all non-Catholics and other religions and it took me some time, once out in the big wide world, to realise that these non-Catholic people were much the same as I. Teachings of this nature are even more extreme in Ireland where they persist to this day causing lack of trust, understanding and violence. If I ever rule the world I will make studies of comparative religion compulsory in all schools and encourage the mixing of religions to ensure greater understanding and tolerance. It is important to realise your neighbour is not someone off the moon and thoroughly understand that religion has caused more wars than anything else in the history of mankind.

Seaside and Holidays

Apart from the annual holiday to the seaside one of the highlights of the summer was the club trip so called because it was usually organised by a working men's club which most men belonged to. The clubs were mostly frequented by men for the cheap beer and entertainment but the seaside trips were for the whole family. In those days before a car appeared in every driveway club trips were an exciting day out and definitely not to be missed. On most trips Dad would be in charge and take the whole family but I recalled on one occasion when he worked on the railways he was actually the fireman on the train taking us to the seaside. It was so exciting as the huge steam train came into the station with Dad waving at us from the cab.As the monster ground to a halt Dads strong arms lifted me up into the cab so that I could see all the dials and levers and feel the heat and see the flames of the boiler. He let me shovel some coal into the boiler and pull the cord which activates the train whistle. I sat on the driver's seat and felt so important looking down at the other children on the platform who were casting envious glances in my direction.

On boarding the train, the smell of cigarette smoke and spilled pale ale was overpowering. Crates of beer were piled high in the walkways between the carriages and excited families were pouring on board laden with drinks and sandwiches trying to find a seat with a table. The two-hour journey passed very quickly with the women exchanging gossip, the men drinking and smoking and excited children playing and running up and down the train. Teenagers were walking up and down the train rather self-consciously looking for potential new boyfriends and girlfriends. When the train finally arrived and chugged into the station people opened windows to drink in the fresh sea air while young lads with homemade barrows lined the platform hoping to transport family luggage to nearby boarding houses in return for a sixpence. The great disembarkation took place with families heading for the beach and teenagers for the rides and amusement arcades. We stopped to see Dad up front in the engine with his white toothed grin shining through his sweaty grimy face as he had been busy feeding the great iron monster with coal during our journey. He would join us on the beach later when the monster had been fueled, watered and parked in a nearby siding ready for the return journey.

Seaside activities were decidedly tacky even by the standards of those days but were a welcome break from a daily grind. Families would head for the beach to enjoy paddling in the sea and building sand castles together with the odd donkey ride or Punch and Judy show. Teenagers headed for the noise and excitement of the rides and amusement arcades to have fun and hopefully form their first friendships with the opposite sex. Boys loved to demonstrate their daring and manly prowess on hair raising rides such as the big dipper and waltzer in the hope of impressing the girls. Men would tend to settle their families on the beach and leave the wife to look after the brood while they tried to find their friends in nearby pubs. Our tired bunch of trippers would reassemble at the station near nightfall and pile on the train again tired but happy. The train thundered through the night on its homeward journey with smoke and sparks flying from its chimney. Dad would be busy shoveling the coal and in the carriages everyone would be enjoying a sing song. Happy days and simple pleasures.

The other bigger treat to look forward to was the annual summer holiday by the seaside usually staying in a variety of self-catering accommodation ranging from caravans to chalets to converted trams. The most popular resorts were around Scarborough, Bridlington and Whitby on the east coast with the occasional foray to Blackpool on the west coast. The east coast was definitely my favourite with its lovely harbours and working fishing boats, nice beaches and interesting cliffs and coves. Breathing in the fresh salty tang of the sea I could go fishing with rod and line from the harbour wall or rocks and eat any fish that I caught. Bigger fish such as cod could be caught by taking a boat out to Flamborough Head with the local fishermen and lowering your line with a heavy weight some one hundred feet down to the sea bottom which was littered with wrecks. The bite of a good sized fish was a real thump and my arm would ache reeling it up from the mysterious depths. The real excitement was seeing it appear in the water as it neared the surface, what size and shape will it be? What species? The glistening silver body would come into view and I said a little prayer that it would not come off the line before it was safely in the boat. The fishermen would deal with it expertly and would gut it and string it for you. When the boat chugged back into the harbour the quay would be crowded with holidaymakers looking down into the boat to see the catch. If, like I, you had a couple of fish to carry off you felt very proud. On return to our holiday accommodation mum would be there to greet me and Dad would prepare the catch for cooking. Never has a fish tasted so good particularly when fried so fresh. I slept well that night dreaming of landing giant cod in great numbers. My favourite holiday locations had to be Whitby and Cayton Bay. Whitby was the home of Captain Cook with a lovely collection of higgledy piggledy cottages clinging to the steep hillsides, most of them with tiny low ceiling rooms in all sorts of odd shapes and fronting narrow little cobbled lanes. The whole town smelled of the sea and fish, gulls wheeled and screeched overhead calling to each other and hoping for titbits as the fishermen unloaded their catches.

There were all sorts of interesting and hidden corners in Whitby, little lanes, hidden courtyards, alleyways leading into secret yards and cottages that were almost impossible to find without local knowledge. No wonder this had once been a smugglers haven. Ancient small pubs were dotted around the lanes with low yellowed ceilings and black and white pictures on the wall of bygone herring fleets and women cleaning the catch in bulky Victorian dresses. The whole place had a rugged and windswept look and seemed to be attached to the sea by its long harbour wall acting as a kind of umbilical cord. The ruined Abbey on the windswept cliff top stood out in stark relief on the headland while the harbour wall with its massive defenses jutted out aggressively to sea.

Real fishermen could be seen everywhere dressed in smocks, mending nets on the harbour side and smoking pipes and exchanging yarns in between bouts of activity. Their eyes twinkled in their weather beaten faces and their rough and gnarled hands were surprisingly quick and adept at repairing the nets. Boxes of freshly caught fish were being unloaded packed with ice, ready for the Market. Boxes of evil looking crabs and lobsters, still alive, were being unloaded for sale. The small stained and battered fishing boats bobbed up and down in the tide, the hulls streaked and rusty, the decks covered with fishing gear, floats, nets, lines and chains. It was hard to see any order among the chaos but the fishermen knew where everything belonged as generations of their forefathers had done before. Whitby had also been a whaling port in the past as evidenced by a huge whalebone monument on the cliff top. What a fascinating town, totally out of the mould, and completely different to any other place I had been. Cayton Bay was quiet and unspoiled when we used to visit, little more than a couple of fields containing a small caravan site with a cleft valley leading down to a lovely beach. I enjoyed many holidays here exploring the beach, beachcombing, looking for crabs and small fish in the rock pools. It never ceases to amaze me what can be found on the beach such as pieces of gnarled and weather beaten wood shaped by the action of the sea to resemble something. Fishermen's cork net floats, shells, bottles, pieces of chain and small rocks with all sorts of colours striped through them are merely a small sample of what could be found. When the tide was out it uncovered all sorts of treasures such as fish trapped in rock pools, crabs taking shelter under rocks, sand eels burying themselves to await the next ride and occasionally larger fish caught in pools by the receding tide. No man made entertainments whatsoever but what a fantastic adventure playground nature had provided, I just loved it!

Harbours

Oh how I loved harbours as a child, the sights, and the smells the activity and the sounds. Whitby, Scarborough and Bridlington all have excellent harbours which are still working harbours and not just havens for pleasure boats and weekend yachtsmen. One daily event I really looked forward to was the return of the fishing boats laden with their catch in the late afternoon.Crab and lobster were landed in crates very much alive with their eyes swiveling and claws moving, boxes of gleaming herring, cod and flatfish were hoisted onto the jetty in ice packed boxes ready for market.

I often would sit on the harbour wall and use my fishing rod to see if I could catch anything for my tea. Fishing inside the harbour would yield small fish and crabs while the sea had bigger fish mostly whiting and flatfish which were good enough for a meal. The sea side did present a greater risk of losing hooks and weights on the weed and rocks.Happy holidaymakers would stroll past looking inquisitively into my bag to see if I had caught anything and would then ask questions on the relative merits of different baits before resuming their evening stroll. Young couples would pass by hand in hand, looking into each other eyes, hypnotized in each other's company, and sharing intimate secrets as only they can. Families passed by with lively and inquisitive young children running around, hands into everything, getting too close to the harbour wall much to the horror of their parents. One little lad, overwhelmed by curiosity, approached the boxes of crabs and touched one on its shell back. As it didn't move he became more confident and approached it again and picked it up. This time it moved rather quickly and nipped him hard on the finger and with an ear piercing yell he dropped the crab but the crab had decided not to drop him. It held on to his finger for a few seconds longer and then dropped off and tried to scuttle away. The tearful and sobbing lad ran for the security of his parents who like other bystanders had already seen the funny side and were laughing their heads off rather unsympathetically.

Smells around the harbour were many and varied, the natural smell of the seaweed exposed by the tide, the pungent smell of bits of discarded fish, the oily smell of a boats exhaust and the fresh smell of the sea breeze supporting the wheeling gulls. Other man made smells abounded, the sickly sweet smell of candy floss eaten by passersby, the pungent smells of hotdogs and onions being cooked at open stalls and by far the best the delicious smell of someone's fish and chips eaten out of the paper as they walked down the Harbour. Seaside fish and chips were always excellent with a bigger than usual piece of fish.

Activities around the Harbour were many and varied. Two

pleasure boats plied their trade; they could take around one hundred people a trip and although old were well maintained. With names such as Coronia and Yorkshire Bell, they would slip easily in and out of the harbour full of happy smiling tourists waving at others on the jetty a few of whom would join in the fun and wave back. An hour cruise to Flamborough Head and back would blow away the cobwebs and ensure a good appetite for the evening meal.Alternatively, if a little exercise was required a rowing boat could be hired to row out of the harbour mouth and perhaps anchor and do a bit of fishing in the open sea.As rowing a boat were the smallest craft using the narrow harbour entrance it could be a little nerve racking returning to base when the harbour was busy. Fishing boats, battered stained and rusty would chug in and out all day long in the eternal pursuit of a catch, handled expertly and effortlessly they would skim the harbour wall missing it by inches and once clear set their course for the fishing grounds. A favourite fishing spot was Flamborough Head a massive white vertical cliff with very deep waters off and some treacherous tides and currents which over the years had attracted many wrecks and was particularly renowned for its cod.

Another type of boat which frequented the harbour was the pleasure fishing boat known as a cobble, mostly open with a small wheelhouse and cabin on the upper deck. These boats would take out eight to ten holiday makers for three-hour fishing trips and it was by far the best way to stand a chance of catching something big. The boat would usually go to the area off Flamborough Head and would anchor in the swells. As with all fishing some days could be slow but other days if the fish were shoaling the action could be fast and furious and some large cod or similar landed.

One fine summer day I sat on the harbour wall fishing and enjoying the sunshine. The sea was like a millpond and a new shape appeared on the horizon.It looked to be smoky grey colour in the summer haze and ahead of it was a large fishing boat of a type I had never seen before. The ships appeared to be moving around each other in a strange nautical dance when all of a sudden there was an enormous bang which took me by surprise and almost made me lose my footing on the harbour wall.I looked up in surprise when I heard a second big bang and could see clouds of smoke around the big fishing boat. It appeared that the grey ship was firing on the fishing boat and for the next half hour or so they both remained stationary on the glassy sea.After a while both ships got underway and appeared to be heading very slowly towards the harbour. Word had now got around on the jungle telegraph and many had heard the bangs. Soon the harbour wall filled up with rubberneckers all anxious to find a good position to watch the action.There was much speculation among the seriously uninformed that the third world war had broken out but a rush for the Daily Mirror showed no such news. The vessels gradually grew bigger and more distinct as they approached the harbour entrance and I realised that the lead ship was a small Royal Navy warship, the first one I had seen in real life.

As they approached the harbour entrance the warship's white ensign fluttered proudly from her stern and I could make out a businesslike gun mounted on the forward part of the ship. The ship's hull and upper works were a uniform grey but immaculately painted and spotlessly clean. I could now make out some of the crew preparing ropes for berthing and several others on the bridge observing the harbour through binoculars. Signal flags in a variety of colours were hoisted in a long flowing stream from the bridge wing to the yardarm on the mast.The ships foghorn emitted several loud blasts to warn smaller craft that she was about to enter harbour. As she performed a gracious curve and lined up to enter I could make out her gleaming brass work and her red and brass nameplate attached to the bridge superstructure, HMS WASPERTON, was a fine sight. The crew, having prepared their berthing ropes, were now stood to attention in single line on stern and focsle.Six in line, shoulders, back in immaculate white shirts and hats proudly displaying the ships name on their cap tallies. These were tough looking characters with chunky forearms emblazoned with tattoos, broad shoulders, some with rather piratical beards and all with a smart confident demeanour. I was spellbound, fishing forgotten, I just stood and stared absorbing every detail of this new experience. The ship slowed and prepared to come alongside the harbour wall, orders were shouted out by the officers on the bridge and the crew prepared their ropes for berthing.

The ship came smoothly alongside and tied up quickly and efficiently, the gangway was rolled out and contact made with terra firma. Ships engines were shut down and silence prevailed with the ship bobbing gently up and down against the harbour wall. Several of the crew quickly disembarked to help tie up the next arrival which turned out to be a Russian trawler which they had arrested for illegal fishing within the twelve-mile limit. Apparently she was less than keen to stop for inspection and was heading out of the twelve-mile limit when a couple of shots across the bow caused her to have a change of mind. The local courts would hear the case the next day and decide the penalty.

The contrast between the two ships was quite pronounced. On the one hand the smart warship with immaculate and efficient crew and on the other the dirty untidy rust streaked Russian trawler with scruffy unshaven and surly crew slouching against the nearest piece of convenient superstructure. The trawler was tied up alongside and immediately Wasperton sent a boarding party of an officer and five sailors armed with sterling sub machine guns on board to take control and prevent any escape during the night. I sat on the side of the harbour wall watching the activity around the ships and some of the crew going on shore leave. Various officials visited the ship and suppliers came on board offering fresh food and replenishment goods. Crowds were milling around as it was unusual to see a warship in such a small harbour. I looked at the ship in more detail, the polished brass, immaculate white wooden deck, the evil looking gun with its rapid load magazine system and polished cone at the end of the barrel. The shell and cartridge was about fifteen inches long and the crew said it could fire one hundred and twenty rounds per minute. As night fell I had to tear myself away and return to our holiday accommodation but as the sun set there was a ceremony on the stern which involved lowering the white ensign to the whistle of the boson's call and immediately after all the ships lights were switched on including a fabulous necklace of coloured lights around the upper deck. As I climbed up above the harbour on my way home the ship looked so impressive and seemed to be competing with the brightly lit amusement arcades on the other side of the harbour.

My loving but slightly anxious mum was waiting for me with a hot meal. Unfortunately, I had not caught any fish that day with all diversions but what new experiences I had enjoyed. I looked out of my bedroom window that night and saw Wasperton in the distant harbour, still brightly lit with figures the size of ants scurrying around the jetty. I watched the activity for some time before sliding into my bed exhausted by the day's excitement and activity and shortly fell into a deep sleep.

Little did I know at the time that in my adult life I would cross paths with HMS WASPERTON again but in totally different circumstances...

Be Prepared

Although my own children regard scouting as rather old fashioned for me at the tender age of eleven it opened up a whole new world of adventure and the feeling of belonging to something really worthwhile. Such was my enthusiasm that I rose rapidly through the ranks to Patrol Leader and eventually Troop Leader at the tender age of seventeen. To me the real magic of scouting was not the weekly meetings of the troop but the beckoning calls the great outdoors and the skills you develop to survive and live comfortably in it. We enthusiastically entered competitions against other scout troops and often walked away with the prize for the best bivouac or bridge across a stream. At the following weeks troop meeting we would proudly carry the trophy in to show our fellow scouts and then replace it in the trophy cupboard for display.

There were many skill tests to go through which earned

different badges which were then sewn on to the uniform shirt. My favourite skill test was known as the backwoodsman which involved building your own shelter for the night and cooking food either caught, or if this was impractical it could be bought.Living in an urban area it did not prove practical to start shooting the Town Hall pigeons and so we bought some from the local butcher and headed for the woods.Once we had selected a good camp site we set about gathering the materials for our bivouac shelter and constructed a frame of branches lashed together with string. This frame was then covered with a deep layer of whatever foliage was available which was usually fern. If the foliage was placed correctly and to the required thickness it was surprisingly waterproof. It was now time to light the fire and construct an improvised spit for pigeon roasting out of green wood which wouldn't burn too easily. The cooking pigeons smelled delicious as they roasted evenly on our spit which we had constructed in such a manner that the birds could be turned. At long last they were ready to eat and provided a meal fit for a king particularly as they had taken longer to cook than we thought and by this stage we were ravenously hungry. After the meal we retired into the bivouac and spent an uneventful night in the company of some rather large spiders and other creepy crawlies.Drifting off to sleep to the accompaniment of all the woodland noises was sheer magic and such a contrast to a town environment. The true test of our creation came with the early morning rainstorm and we remained remarkably dry with our fern covering

The annual scout camp week, involving the whole troop was the highlight of the summer which everyone looked forward to.One year we stayed on a farm near Scarborough which was very nice in itself but it had the misfortune to border a rubbish tip inhabited by large numbers of giant rats.

We were rather worried that they would pay us a nocturnal visit in search of food and therefore we decided to arrange a preemptive strike. We gathered together a few highly illegal catapults and air guns and marched off to the tip. If we moved quietly we found, we could get quite close to the rats as they were preoccupied searching for food among the rubbish. We managed to dispatch quite a few to ratty heaven that afternoon and we discovered that rats are not particularly proud when it comes to eating as the survivors started to eat the less fortunate ones. It did have the effect of keeping them away from the camp however as they had plenty of former friends to consume.

On another of the annual camps we stayed in a farmer's field near Aberford which was fairly isolated apart from a convenient pub a few fields away. The toilet tent was discreetly positioned in a small low lying wooded area nearby and holes were dug to last the week together with support and safety rails to ensure no one fell in and became an instant social outcast. There was something decidedly odd about this place although at first sight it was just a small copse of trees with rooks nesting in them and a tangle of brambles and undergrowth at ground level. Even venturing in to the place alone during the daytime as one did to go to the toilet gave everyone a feeling of unease as if being watched. At night, despite the urgency of the mission, no one would venture in alone as the place was so sinister. Apart from the rooks there was no sign of life, no birdsong, no rustlings of rabbits in the undergrowth, just total silence. One night our scoutmaster offered anyone six beers if they would spend thirty minutes in the wood alone but there were no takers, which was hardly surprising.

We made some investigations into the history of this area

and came up with some rather alarming facts and folklore. Apparently the fields had been a battleground during the Wars of the Roses and local folklore stated the copse had been used

As a burial ground for both humans and horses as it was damp, low lying and useless for agriculture. We also began to notice that our friendly farmer never ventured into the area which lent some credence to the story. The landlord of the local pub was also a bit of a local historian and he mentioned in passing that the anniversary of the battle fell during our stay. He also mentioned that some ghostly headless knight also rode along some of the pathways in the area and that several locals had seen him on the anniversary of the battle. Apparently this knight was racing back to tell of the recent victory when a cowardly knight hid in a tree above the path and decapitated him as he rode past. This was too good to miss so we obtained directions to this pathway, took our sleeping bags and hid in a ditch all night in the hope of seeing the headless knight. Fortified by a couple of beers we peered anxiously into the swirling mists and took turns to sleep somewhat fitfully. After a while on watch we started to imagine shapes and figures in the mist but nothing positive was seen that night and we returned to camp cold and stiff at first light but with our enthusiasm for mysteries undiminished. In fact, so brave did we feel that we walked through the corpse on the way back drawing strength from each other to help overcome our fear but the sinister menace of the place seemed to have disappeared on this fine morning and a strange stillness prevailed. It was almost as if you could sense the dead beneath your feet at rest once more on the anniversary of their battle. By the following day the old sense of grim foreboding had returned with a vengeance and the copse was silent and sinister save for the mournful cry of the rooks in their lofty lair.

One of the most enjoyable aspects of scouting was night time escape and evasion games between different patrols with the objective of escape or attack. A number of us became very good at this hugging the contours of the land with our bodies, blacking out faces and taking an age to cross a few yards of open terrain. These skills became very useful on one occasion when we were camped close to a girl guides camp.In the first instance we went across to the girl guides camp to introduce ourselves and the troop as good manners would dictate and we were met with rabid suspicion and almost open hostility by the adults in the party both male and female.We were taken aback by this reception as scouting is normally such a friendly organisation but they had made it clear that they wanted nothing to do with us and we were aggrieved by this attitude.

On the first night we therefore decided to have a bit of fun probing and testing the enemy defenses to see how close we could get without being detected. We often lay in hiding just a few feet away listening to the usual girly chatter and who fancies who boyfriend and girlfriend relationships which occupy so much girl time. After a while we got bored and crept out into the night to try something else.The real evasion top guns now decided to try the ultimate challenge of entering a tent between tent bottom and groundsheet while the girls were occupied elsewhere by food or other activities. To establish success, it was necessary to leave a souvenir such as a fancy knot in a short length of rope or a carved stick on top of or just inside a convenient sleeping bag to cause some alarm and trepidation at bed time.To prove you had made the objective to your peers in the group it was necessary to return with evidence such as a stocking, hair slide or for the perfect ten score and the lasting admiration of your peers, a pair of knickers!

The big night in the guide's female only calendar was the camp fire night which the organisers tried to keep female only as in their eyes any kind of contact with the opposite sex was out of bounds at this tender age. As our presence was positively discouraged we felt duty bound to spice things up by mounting a suitable covert operation.Our first task was to send out spies to gather intelligence on their plans and proposals. On their return our planning and ideas group would meet to come up with ideas and eventually a plan would materialise.

The ingenuity of a good scout group armed with nothing more than string, wood and a few household items are nothing short of legendary. Our spies had discovered the camp fire would be held in a disused quarry forming a natural amphitheater with the old quarry cliff face on one side and gently sloping rock strewn banks on the other sides. The rocky terrain and a few trees in the vicinity offered excellent cover.

We commenced our preparations in the late afternoon. While one group kept an eye on the girl's camp another group rigged ropes up in the trees and hid them from view in the foliage. Meanwhile back in our camp others had made the body of a witch out of twigs, straw and old items of clothing. Someone had even managed to make a large conical paper Mache hat.Others had managed to make evil looking masks out of hollowed out pumpkins acquired from our friendly farmer. After the girls had finished their evening meal they began to run over to the quarry and milled around like a group of excited foals.

The fire was duly lit and they settled down to tell stories and sing songs. We gave them about an hour to warm up and then put stage one of our plan into action. We had a group running around some distance from the quarry making ghostly and wolf like noises during breaks in the singing. Our audience started to look around and stare into the inky blackness but could see nothing and became a little apprehensive. Stage two was now implemented and consisted of four others a little closer to the quarry running round draped in white sheets with torches below. They looked spooky but could not be seen too accurately at the distance. The audience gave forth a number of nervous screams and started to look a little restless when our next group hidden in the cliff face of the quarry lit the candles in their grotesque pumpkin masks and placed them strategically so that they could be observed but not seen too clearly. By now there was a bit of panic in the audience and we were laughing our heads off and waiting for the grand finale. To keep the momentum going we brought this forward by a few minutes and this one really sowed the seeds of terror when our model witch, with lantern in hand, swung from one tree to another at the opposite end of the quarry. To the sound of a blood curdling scream and cackle she described an almost perfect arc above the fire with her feet almost brushing the coals before she disappeared up the opposite tree.

The end result was fantastic and exceeded all our expectations causing total panic and a headlong rush back to the camp site. However even in camp the poor girls were not safe as another of our groups had infiltrated their tents and left a few presents in sleeping bags. A fascinating collection of frogs, toads, snails, worms and even a couple of friendly hedgehogs had been left to keep them company. We returned to camp doubled up and almost ill with laughter, opened a beer or two and reflected on how well the evening had gone.

On Yer Bike

Cycling opened up a whole new world for me, I suppose the addiction started at thirteen and lasted until I was sixteen when I graduated to my first moped. It gave me great freedom and independence and enabled me to escape from my grimy town and into the countryside.My uncle gave me my first adult bike which was an old wreck but nevertheless it had a lightweight racing frame and great potential to be restored and rebuilt. After much scraping together of cash over the long winter months a freshly painted Saxon reborn with new wheels and tyres and other accessories emerged from the garden shed and into the light of day

A school friend, Anthony, was also a keen cyclist and we started the tradition of the Sunday run, weather permitting. Initially we covered about fifty miles a day but by the end of the summer we were exceeding one hundred miles per day. I had a little mechanical mileometer attached to my front wheel and the target for each Sunday soon became one hundred miles or more.

We would pore over the map and try to select a different route and destination for each run and where possible we would try to include some of the smaller less well known roads which were likely to have less traffic and more interest. We would leave the smoke and grime of Dewsbury behind, head for Bradford which was even worse, but once on the other side of the city the gateway to the dales began to open with its lovely rolling countryside, dry stone walls, grazing sheep and rushing streams.

We started off modestly with the nearest places of interest such as Ilkley, Otley and Skipton and gradually moved further out to Ingleton, Settle, Gargrave and Knaresborough. The trips would commence about nine in the morning with a vigorous ride to the other side of Bradford and then a stop for tea from the flask and a hefty sandwich, most welcome after a twenty-five mile ride.

Lunchtime would normally see us at our destination cycling around and exploring the chosen town or village. For lunch we would have the remainder of the sandwiches and tea usually sat by a stream or river, cooling our feet in the rushing waters. An hour or so for rest and then time to head back arriving home around seven in the evening feeling tired, incredibly hungry and really fit. The fantastic charge of fresh air seemed to benefit us for the remainder of the week. In those days I thought nothing of cycling eight or ten miles to school or to see a friend.

Cycling was then a very popular sport with terrific comradeship and many cycling clubs available to join. It was great fun cycling through the countryside on some of the minor roads and as bikes made very little noise we often surprised rabbits, pheasants and other birds that had not picked up on our silent approach. Birds would swoop and soar around us; the air was incredibly fresh and pure apart from in the vicinity of farmyards. Spirits would soar as we tackled the elements and battled through gusty winds and the odd rain shower.

Return to town was always slightly depressing for although it had facilities the countryside lacked it could not compete with the sheer natural delight of countryside. We would cross the urban grime as quickly as possible on our way home trying to find steep hills to get up speed and overtake unsuspecting Reliant three wheeler motor cars. We would often return with a small clump of heather or bunch of wild flowers attached to the handlebars and would carefully pre-serve these for the rest of the week as a reminder of our Sunday journey.

Margaret was my First Love

And she was in my class as the popular song goes. When I was thirteen going out with girls was simply not done and anyone who tried was subject to taunts and ridicule by the peer group who would look down on you for letting down the macho image.Any relationship that developed had therefore to remain discrete, and so it was with Margaret. She was a cute little thing of medium height, a pair of rather fetching pigtails, a face full of freckles, budding rosebud breasts and a rather cheeky smile.

We both enjoyed swimming and would arrange to meet some Saturday mornings by passing discrete messages either from hand to hand when passing in the school corridor or if no one was around whispered arrangements in some quiet corner. It was all very conspiratorial and, like most things forbidden, quite exciting. The relationship was purely platonic sealed with a cup of Bovril after swimming.

Although we lived in adjacent towns and therefore never visited each other at home we also used to meet each other occasionally at ballroom dancing lessons. I really used to enjoy dancing lessons and unlike modern dancing you could hold a girl close and have a pleasant conversation with music set at a reasonable volume. The only problem was that the instructor paired you off with a partner at the start and I would often have to gaze at Margaret from the other side of the room. We enjoyed the waltz quickstep and cha cha all summer long but sadly all good things come to an end. We grew up a bit more and went our separate ways, the drift apart encouraged by the fact that we both started working Saturdays, Margaret in a shop and myself on the local market.

I often wondered what had happened to Margaret and didn't see her for many years until I finally managed to make my first school reunion some thirty years after I left! As I entered the room some of my former classmates had changed totally while others had not and I could recognise them immediately. Margaret was in this latter category and I recognised her immediately standing

Chatting in a small group but alas without the pigtails. She looked over and smiled at me as she did all those years ago but her impish smile had faded a little no doubt due to the hard knocks of life. It was nice to chat to her again after so many years but we quickly realised that we had developed in our own and very opposite ways and we now had little in common. She had spent most of her life as a social worker in her home town whereas I had travelled and worked all over the world.

Next on the girlfriend scene was Susan, she was somewhat more sophisticated than Margaret and definitely more worldly. She was older than her years suggested, dressed very stylishly and often went out with older boys. She had beautiful long dark hair, slim figure and long shapely legs.I took her to the cinema a couple of times where we occupied the back seats with all the other couple's intent on getting to know each other better. She was quite enthusiastic in the kissing and cuddling game and was quite happy to let my hand wander into her blouse to caress her small but perfectly formed breasts. I suppose at that time I thought taking a girl to the cinema was the height of sophistication but Susan was older than her age suggested and was used to going into pubs with older lads who sometimes had cars.I could not compete with that and at the tender age of fourteen certainly did not look old enough to get into a pub. As a result, our relationship did not last long as I found her conversation somewhat limited and she probably regarded me as just too young.

I liked a girl I went to school with who lived about half a mile away on the end of our road.Her name was Christine and I would see her almost every day as we waited for the school bus. In the spring time before we sat our O level exams she managed to persuade respective mothers that it would be a good idea if we studied together in the evenings and helped each other with any difficulties. By the time I got to know what was going on everything had been agreed and the motherly seal of approval given.As she had a very inquisitive younger sister who appeared to like me a lot she also arranged to come to our house to study. This arrangement began to grow on me as Christine was a blue eyed blonde with nice legs and I knew the only place we could study in peace in our crowded house was my bedroom.She duly arrived looking very attractive but still in school uniform and we went up to my simply furnished room where the only place we could sit was on my bed. We made a good start to the studying and did help each other quite a lot but I did find it increasingly difficult to concentrate on fascinating topics such as algebra and calculus while Christine's pert young breasts were rising and falling through her modest blouse in time with her breathing. We were sitting shoulder to shoulder and I could smell the softness of her and the warmth of her body raising my passion by the minute. However, I had to be careful as the morality police, in the form of my mother, was nearby. I heard her familiar tread on the staircase and from long practice knew which stair she had just trodden on by its distinctive creak. Mother came in to check on us carrying a couple of glasses of lemonade as an excuse for her appearance and once she had taken her leave we closed the math's books and decided a practical biology lesson would be infinitely more educational and much more fun. Christine enjoyed herself so much she used to come along three times a week and both families were deeply impressed with our commitment to study. At the end of each study session I would walk her home via the local cemetery where in a quiet corner we could practice some more.So passed a pleasant Spring and Summer for the joint study was certainly beneficial in more ways than one, I passed nine O levels later that year.

Did I see Christine again, not for many years but she married, had children and seems very content and fulfilled.

When I started working on Saturdays and in the summer holidays I began to meet a different type of girl from the schoolgirl or student with whom I was familiar. I began to meet shop girls and mill girls who were around my place of work and typically these girls left school at sixteen with no qualifications. They usually went directly to the mill often to train as weavers and there they would stay until an enterprising young man came along and pregnancy and a shotgun marriage would be the normal outcome.Several years and children down the line they ended up as fat bored housewives who had lost their looks, living in a rented terrace house round the corner from the mill.Such was life's rich and predictable pattern that most young girls would make the best of their carefree teenage years of happy go lucky freedom. Many of these girls were by no means thick but they often came from home backgrounds opposed to education and suspicious of upward mobility above ones' pre-ordained station in life.

Glenys was a typical example of the breed, a pretty looking girl I met in my local pub and went out with on and off for several months. She was a couple of years older than I and was going out at the same time with another older lad. I wasn't supposed to know about him but I did.My original idea in going out with her was that she was a couple of years older and therefore I assumed more sophisticated and wise to the ways of the world. We would usually go to the pub followed by the cinema where Glenys liked to settle down and enjoy a kiss and a cuddle like most girls.One particular night I could sense that she was feeling really hot so I thought the way might be clear to go a little further than usual and see what the reaction was. We settled down in our seats and after the usual preliminaries she was well and truly warmed up. I particularly like the fact that she was wearing a very short skirt which was in danger of riding up with our physical exertions and revealing the Promised Land. I draped my coat over both our laps and moved my hand gently onto her knee under my coat.She looked into my eyes approvingly her hot chewing gum breath caressing my cheek and her breathing started to quicken. Encouraged by her reaction I slowly moved my hand up her smooth silky stocking, her legs parted slightly to accommodate me, until I touched that most erotic area of hot creamy thigh above the stocking top which I squeezed and caressed.Her breathing quickened and became a little noisy, she looked into my eyes again and opened her legs to welcome me further and I could feel her heat. As things were now reaching a crucial stage I looked anxiously around the cinema to see if anyone was watching but everyone seemed to be engrossed in the film or their own liaisons. Glenys willed me on with her eyes and I caressed her through her pants and could feel the heat and moistness beyond. I moved her pants to one side and stroked the mass of moist hair which made her moan softly. My exploring fingers slid easily up her moist tunnel of love and she groaned and whispered my name.Her hand slid under the coat and caressed my manhood and she

Then unzipped and plunged her soft little hand into my trousers feeling and exploring.

We suddenly realised the film was coming to an end and therefore hastily rearranged ourselves and sat there innocently awaiting the lights coming on. On my way home I savoured the distinctive sweet scent of a woman for the first time. Sadly, I never saw Glenys again, she may have thought things were getting too serious or complicated and had been forced to choose but it suited me as I had no desire to be tied down at such a young age. I heard later that she may have moved with her family to another town. Oh where are you now I wonder?

Christine was similar in many ways to Glenys, about a year older than me, bottle blonde with pale complexion who also worked in the mill. She had a pretty face but when you looked upon her you realised it may not stand the test of time. She often came into my local with friends and lived about a mile from my place. I would often catch the last bus from town with her or see her on it if she had been out with friends. I would usually volunteer to walk her home to ensure her safety and depending on the state of her relations with her mother I would be invited in or not. Her mother seemed to like me but she was often at loggerheads with her daughter.

Like many women Christine was fairly unpredictable her actions being determined primarily by where she was in her monthly cycle. Sometimes she didn't really want to know men, other times she was frightened to death about pregnancy and occasionally she was red hot which was the time I liked to meet her most. One cold night we couldn't go in as she had fallen out with her mother yet again but she was hot for sex so we tried it standing up next to the kitchen door. I had never realised how difficult this could be in the freezing cold with Christine several inches shorter than me and wearing a tight skirt.

Undoubtedly the best night we had was another cold winter's night when she was hot and her mother welcomed us in to a roaring fire and promptly went to bed. We settled down on the rug in front of the fire safe in the knowledge that her mother, the only other occupant of the house, never ventured downstairs once she had retired. Three and a half hours later I crawled out happy but exhausted to make my way home with suspected burns to my rear end from being too close to the fire. Unfortunately, after this tryst Christine became very serious and rather unhappy when she learned I was off to join the Royal Navy which was a convenient escape route as it turned out.

Trouble at T'Mill, Mr. Sykes

Once I was sixteen I could legally work full time as an adult and started to look for a student summer job to earn some cash for a holiday. At sixteen the mill was one of the options as you had to be eighteen to be a postman or bus conductor which were the two most sought after and best paid student jobs.I caught a rumour that a small mill in Batley was looking for staff so I cycled the three miles and called in to see them. The place was indeed quite small by mill standards with a long cobbled yard dividing the two main buildings and a ground floor office just inside the yard. The buildings were two storeys of dirty and discoloured stone under a blue slate roof. There were a number of other mills in the vicinity plus the usual jumble of workers terraced houses, pubs and corner shops. I knocked on the door of the office and slowly entered to be greeted by a helpful girl with a nice smile which I did my best to return.Her three workmates in the office also looked up and smiled warmly, I suppose I was a distraction from the routine boredom of clerical work. The girls asked me a surprising number of very direct questions such as, where do you live? do you have a girlfriend? until I almost thought I was being interviewed by them.

All this female attention was a little overwhelming but as I was to find out later girls in the mill were a law unto themselves and bound by few conventions. At this point the boss appeared and I was summoned to his office. My groundwork with the girls may have paid off as one of them nipped in before me and may have put in a good word for me.

I ventured in to his oak paneled office which was quite luxurious in comparison with the rest of the mill. This was my first experience of power as Mr. Sykes was not only the boss but also the owner. I didn't really know what to expect but I found him very easy to converse with and interested in the subjects I was studying.A knock on the door and my newly found friend came in with a lovely smile and tea in two fine china cups. Once she had put the tea down she looked towards me and gave a mischievous little wink and smile, the gleam in her eyes perhaps promising more than tea. I returned the smile with what I hoped would pass for a sophisticated and knowing glance.

After tea Mr. Sykes relaxed a little and launched into his standard speech about working hard and the dangers of machinery, he then declared the job was mine.It was for eight weeks to cover the summer holiday period at four pounds fifty pence per week commencing at eight thirty the following Monday morning. After many thanks and the usual pleasantries I took my leave via the girls in the office who were keen to know how I had got on. Shirley was the girl with the smile and she walked me down the yard towards the gates and gave my hand a soft moist squeeze on parting. I knew that I would see much more of Shirley before the summer was over.

Monday morning dawned and I set off bright and early on my bike with a box of sandwiches specially prepared by my mother.Pedalling through the morning drizzle I felt a little apprehensive about how a sixteen-year-old student would fit in or be accepted.Would I be accepted as a fellow worker; would I be regarded as a boss's plant or worst of all as I did not have a very broad Yorkshire accent would I be considered "posh". I need not have worried too much as Northern folk call a spade a spade, they will soon point out any shortcomings but at the same time are welcoming if you try to fit in.

I parked my bike and knocked on the door on the mill office which was opened almost immediately by my friend Shirley.Her smile was every more radiant than before and tinged with that delightful element of hidden promise.She smelled strongly but sweetly of perfume or talcum powder and was well dressed even for an office girl who was always considered themselves a social grade above the other women in the mill who were usually weavers.She moved her face close to mine as if to kiss but I was shy and a little confused by the signals and insufficiently experienced in body language at the time.Nevertheless, Shirley had a strong and profound effect on me, the thought of her attentions excited me as she had a raw and earthy quality to her. I went in to the office and submitted to the critical inspection of her friends who were all smiles with occasional sideways glances at Shirley to give her encouragement.

I was ushered into Mr. Sykes office to an authoritative but fatherly welcome.Much to my short term embarrassment

Mr. Sykes and I had hit it off and he therefore decided to give me a tour of the mill to explain the functions of all the departments before starting work.Kind gesture though this was it immediately marked me out as some form of managerial plant or even worse a relative of the owner. This took about two weeks and a lot of hard work to live down although the tour itself was fascinating. Undoubtedly the most impressive part was the weaving shed populated in the main by young women. The place was incredibly noisy and dusty with adept women performing strange tasks with skillful hands involving shuttles and looms.The strangest custom in the weaving shed was speaking in sign language due to the noise of the machines. What I didn't know but every other man did was that, despite seeming to be absorbed in their work, these women never missed anything and the presence of a new young man gave rise to a chorus of wolf whistles and associated gestures of an intimate nature.The whistles could be heard above the incredibly noise machinery and I wished the floor to open and swallow me up, such was my embarrassment.

Having escaped from the weavers shed I realised I may not be quite so lucky next time when not accompanied by Mr. Sykes! We continued our journey across the yard to the finishing shed where the heavy woollen worsted cloth was pressed, folded, packed and dispatched to destinations all over the world.This was where I would work for the next eight weeks. We ran through some of the destination labels which really fired my emerging wanderlust, Ottawa, Peking, Nepal, Chicago and Christchurch New Zealand. If you need to keep warm, British worsted was the best, would last half a lifetime and our mill specialised in making it. Mr. Sykes introduced me to the supervisor and took his leave whereupon the supervisor took me across to Herbert as I was to be his work partner for the first week. When I first saw Herbert I had to swallow hard in disbelief, the poor sod looked just like the hunchback of Notre Dame; he could have acted the part without make up or padding. He was stooped, twisted, had only two teeth and a very convincing hump. Just in case nature had thought to be over generous in the allocation of good looks she had also given him a funny shrivelled hand and a club foot. I was horrified and speechless at the same time. I just had no idea how to react to a situation like this. Herbert reached out offering his good hand and smiled at me revealing his two solitary teeth which looked to be the size of gravestones in his otherwise empty mouth. He even had a twisted smile to complete his totally revolting appearance.

I gradually got used to Herbert as I worked with him over the next few weeks and found him to be one of the nicest and kindest people you could ever wish to meet, truly confirming the old maxim that appearances can be deceptive.

Even in my student days I quickly realised the problems which lay ahead for the mill industries. Much of the equipment I worked with was dated 1897 and although strong and durable had changed little since that date. The most modern machine in the mill had been built in 1937. It did not need a genius to know that before long the industry would be eclipsed by competition from the third world using more modern machinery.

I set to work with Herbert with great gusto keen to earn my wages. Our first task was to operate the pressing machine which consisted of two enormous rollers through which all the finished cloth had to be fed prior to folding and packing. Using this machine required the utmost manual dexterity and concentration. The rollers pressed together with a force of eight tons and although there was a safety stop bar it would not stop the rollers immediately due to their weight and momentum.Herbert watched over me with almost fatherly concern but I had no desire to lose an arm up to the elbow so I kept vigilant. The really tricky bit was starting a new length of heavy cloth on the roller as you had to get it high up to stay on the roller usually only inches from where the two rollers met.

Apart from Herbert there were one or two other interesting characters in the all-male finishing shed.Eric was a rather timid and somewhat harmless middle aged homosexual of the effeminate variety but otherwise inoffensive.He used to potter around at low speed on his beloved motor scooter wobbling rather dangerously and giving everyone in sight the presidential wave.Unfortunately, his concentration on the road was somewhat wanting and he was always having minor accidents and near misses.

Marty on the other hand was a tough looking Elvis Presley fan who modelled his appearance on the early version of his idol.Marty had been round the clock twice. He often used to entertain us with somewhat explicit stories of his activities with the ladies, some probably for real and others made up.He certainly seemed to know plenty of women but the ones I saw him with were definitely at the lower end of the market. He always dressed in jeans and jeans jacket although he looked a bit like a teddy boy and I could imagine him in long jacket and drainpipe trousers.

John was the other real character of medium height and build and about forty years of age. He was a complex character, a mother's boy who still lived at home and had never married. After a few weeks he seemed to become jealous and resentful of my acceptance within the group and kept insulting me for no apparent reason.I just shrugged this off at first as I needed the job and knew I would only be there for a few weeks. Eventually John went over the top during a cigarette break near the toilet and Marty insisted I exact retribution or he would. This was difficult for me as I am not naturally violent but most of all I didn't wish to lose my hard won job. At the same time however I did not wish to lose the respect of my peers and John had more than deserved his reward. A couple of quick hard thumps to the body leaving no visible marks and a warning of dire consequences if he continued his bad habits did the trick and I retained my credibility. Thankfully and much to my relief John was no hero and kept his mouth shut after that episode.

My best achievement in gaining acceptance happened completely by accident but I was quick to take advantage of it. Lunch time in the mill was called dinner time and normally consisted of ten minutes to eat sandwiches and the rest of the hour sat on smelly bales with sporadic conversation around the Daily Mirror, sport, sex and the odd bit of politics. The only excitement came with the constant need for vigilance against marauding gangs of weaving shed women who would search out new and young men in particular for exotic mill initiation ceremonies and the newer and younger you were the more you were at risk. Usually the marauding groups were eight or so strong and the basic idea was to catch the hapless victim, strip him and finally apply liberal amounts of black boot polish to his private parts. In order to counter this very real threat we planned escape routes through the bales of finished cloth and created special hiding places within the bales for use in extremis. By using these techniques, I managed to evade three marauding gangs and was never caught. This training proved very useful later in the military!

Standard reading after dinner was the Daily Mirror which was hardly an intellectual challenge but I used to bring a book in. Herbert, who wasn't a big reader, asked me to read a bit of the book out loud to him so I did and very soon found I had an audience. I quickly realised that I had made a staggering discovery using my own education as a benchmark I automatically assumed that everyone else was a competent reader. I was humbled to realise that the majority of these lovely people could only read haltingly on a word for word basis. I asked them at the end of the first reading session if they had enjoyed it and if they would like me to read to them again. The answer was a resounding yes. I then asked them if they liked poetry, history, novels or whatever. Poetry was a popular choice so on my way home I popped into the library and borrowed a couple of books.

The following day we tried poems by Keats, Shelley, Rupert Brooke and Wilfred Owen. I tried to read slowly with much passion as I could and was amazed to find them spellbound. They were completely silent with hardly a cough or a movement as they absorbed this new world beyond the Daily Mirror. Word spread, the audiences grew a little bigger and even one or two of the weaving shed girls were allowed in on the promise of good behaviour and no boot polish. Occasionally I was asked to explain part or all of a poem and as a sixteen-year-old orator I did my best. Some of the men shed a tear without embarrassment at the beauty of some works and particularly at the horror of the First World War poems no doubt remembering so many fine fathers and uncles who had cheerfully set off to fight, never to return to their native land even in death. Even Mr. Sykes popped his head around the door one day to see what was going on. I saw him out of the corner of my eye but he just smiled and left us undisturbed.

I was always looking for new material and one day decided to try out some love poems on the weaving shed girls with a bit of animation thrown in to amuse the rest of the audience. Before I started the poem I selected a couple of young pretty and attentive ones sat at the front for the special attention. I would look into their eyes and almost recite the poem to them alone. When we came to parts where the lover holds his ladies hand and strokes her hair I did the same so add effect and it certainly did. The girls blushed and looked away but you could tell they secretly loved it while the rest of the audience fell around laughing. The result was very encouraging and if I had stayed in the mill for longer I am sure several girls would have volunteered for private readings!

Pleased that I had completed another week at the mill and with my pay packet in my pocket I strolled down the yard to retrieve my bike for the journey home. Row after row of bikes were parked in the shed and not one of them was locked up but they were never stolen in those days. My bike, rebuilt from my uncle's old wreck, had a very unusual racing frame and as I wheeled it out I passed two girls who had smart racing machines. We started chatting and they asked me some questions about mine. Elizabeth and Maureen were sisters who worked together in the weaving shed and were also keen weekend cyclists like myself. They invited me to go on a summer evening bike ride with them on the next fine evening. With a hint of mischief in their eyes they explained that they always did everything together and were inseparable. About a week later the weather was good so after a wash and brush up we set off through Bradford and out towards Skipton stopping to purchase sandwiches and lemonade en route. It was one of those beautiful summer evenings with perfect hot weather, no wind and the promise of a magnificent sunset. We rode through Skipton and out towards some farms where we found a ripening cornfield and concealed ourselves and bikes in it to enjoy our picnic.It was a perfect evening but I suspected there was even more to come for I knew the sisters had other things on their mind. Whenever we had stopped on the journey they had been sure to get as close as possible and act in a sexy and provocative manner. They told me earlier they shared everything in life and now they wanted to share me! We lay down in the sweet smelling corn and started to kiss and caress, it was so incredibly mind blowing and exciting. One was kissing me passionately while the other was undoing my shirt, button by button, and kissing and massaging my chest.My hands caressed one sister's generous breasts and lovely moist things and then they would change places so that I could enjoy the other sister. Eventually as the sun went down we retrieved our clothing strewn around the corn and set off on our journey home. What an experience, I hardly had the energy left to cycle home!

I somehow had to keep the sisters discreet as I was still seeing Shirley but I need not have worried as they were discretion itself, not even bragging about their conquest in the weaving shed but keeping it as their own sisterly secret. Mill girls, like many others, enjoyed the short butterfly years of youth before having children, piling on weight and losing their looks.It's such a pity that youth cannot last forever and trysts in cornfields are available on demand, not just one off memories.

The warm summer weeks rolled by and my days at the mill became rather boring. The mind numbing repetition of work made me realise that if I had been destined for a lifetime in the mill it would have driven me crazy. I had been out quite a few times with the lovely Shirley, five-foot three inches tall with an elfin smile and short blonde hair. She was a lovely girl and

I liked her a lot but I knew our paths would diverge shortly and it was very difficult to tell her. We had been out to the cinema, the park and coffee bars which were just becoming fashionable and had kissed and cuddled enthusiastically.She had even let me squeeze and kiss her beautiful pert young breasts. I had deliberately tried not to take things further because like so many other young women she had started to get a little serious and possessive. When she eventually discovered my sights were set on travel and far horizons her interest began to fade particularly when I mentioned I was hitch hiking and camping to France after finishing at the mill.She had also somehow found out about my cycling trip with the sisters and was not too happy although ultimately forgiving. She was a lovely girl and I hope that she has now found happiness with a new man.

At last my eight weeks at the mill were up and I said my farewells to the finishing department, the reading group and all my new found friends. We promised to stay in touch but I was about to move to a new world and we never did so. I reached an accommodation with Shirley and said my goodbyes with a bit of a heavy heart for she was a lovely girl. I gave the fun loving sisters a bit of a squeeze for old times' sake and we recalled all the fun we had had. I had my farewell cup of tea with Mr. Sykes, thanked him for his help, shook the dust off my feet, got the smell of the mill out of my clothes and contemplated the next big adventure!

The French Connection

After leaving the mill, Gerry a school friend, and I decided to have a couple of week's holiday hitch hiking and camping in France before the start of the next school term. At the tender age of sixteen this was quite an adventure and gave my mother several sleepless nights although Dad thought it was a great idea. My uncle who was a lorry driver had offered to take us to London and we met him early one Sunday morning on a roundabout near Wakefield. Ray arrived just a few minutes after the agreed time and we packed rucksacks and ourselves into the warmth of his cab for the long journey. Just over four hours later Ray dropped us in north London and we managed to cross London by nightfall by a combination of walking and local buses. As we were still in the south London suburbs at nightfall we could find nowhere to camp so we unpacked our sleeping bags and dossed down on the bench in a bus shelter. The following morning, we awoke to find ourselves surrounded by a crowd of inquisitive early morning commuters who regarded us with rabid suspicion probably thinking we were junior meth's drinkers or something.

By the evening of day two we were approaching Dover after obtaining a variety of short lifts, the most memorable one being in a lovely old MG Saloon with leather upholstery driven by a middle aged homosexual banker. I could tell he was that way inclined as he repeatedly tried to change gear with my right knee. Perhaps he was just being a little adventurous or maybe brave as Gerry and I carried a wicked looking sheath knife each strapped to our belts. Viva la difference as the French say. Once in Dover we found that the only camp site available was full so we left the town and decided to camp rough. We climbed towards the white cliffs and found a wide ledge upon which we pitched the tent.After a pleasant evening consuming the ubiquitous tinned stew we turned in only to be awakened the following morning by a large and officious man who told us we couldn't camp here as it was Ministry of Defence Property. We did point out to Mr. Pompous that if he was correct there was distinct lack of signs to inform the public that this was the case and eventually he went away muttering into his beard. We then struck camp and headed down to the ferry terminal and boarded the next ferry finding a seat on the stern to take advantage of the bright sunny morning. Ropes were slipped and the ferry glided out of the harbour majestically on a calm sea. As the white cliffs of Dover receded in the distance little did I know that my early career would be bound up with ships and the sea.

The cranes of Calais dock came into view and our excitement mounted. Not only was it the first time we had left England but it was also our first holiday without parents or scout group.We eventually disembarked and gazed at the unfamiliar surroundings, cars travelling on the other side of the road, strange smells, different shop fronts and the general hub bub in a foreign tongue. We had both studied French at school and had enough of the language to get by on, now was the time to put theory into practice. We decided to get the local bus to Boulogne where we knew of a campsite in nearby Wimereux. We arrived in the late afternoon and found the site was quite a big one full of many different nationalities which was exactly what we were looking for. One thing about traveling light with everything on your back is that unpacking and pitching a two-man tent takes only a few minutes. In a similar vein creating a tasty stew from the tin takes only a few minutes more.

After nightfall we decided to explore the delights of Boulogne. After a few false starts we hit upon a friendly little bar up a side street off the promenade. These bars were usually fairly quiet when compared to an English pub but there were a few young people around and we decided to try to liven it up a bit. One of our favourite records on the juke box was the moving Russian song "Kalina" and Gerry and I decided to do our usual Cossack dance to it. Squatting on our haunches and kicking legs straight out one at a time is visually impressive but physically exhausting. The pace quickened as we described a circle and increased leg speed by using alternate hand support. Very soon we had our own audience singing along and clapping in time to the music with the bar becoming lively and some young French men having a go without realising initially just how difficult it is. The dance is so physically demanding we could only repeat it six times a night even with complimentary beers and rest in between.

The enthusiastic audience, clapping away, drove us to new heights and we would throw ourselves around like dervishes.

It was during one of these mad moments when I first noticed Marie, a pretty little French girl, typically Northern France stock, medium height, slightly stocky build and long tresses of shiny black hair. When the dance was over I looked at her again and smiled, she smiled back, looked me straight in the eyes and then modestly averted her gaze. I walked across to talk to her, pretty little Marie Therese Labous was around seventeen and could speak a few words of English to help my schoolboy French. She lived in Wimereux and worked in a shoe shop in Boulogne and we got on like a house on fire sharing the same outlandish sense of humour and the ability to laugh at most things. We had a drink and held hands, chatting away intimately until the bar closed.

We walked out into the warm summer night and along the promenade watching ships going in and out of the harbour and lights twinkling on the shoreline. It was too perfect an evening to go home and we strolled, arm in arm, feeling a growing bond of intimacy between us and some anticipation of where the night would take us. We moved down to walk on the beach stopping every few yards to kiss and embrace with increasing passion and intensity. We reached an area with a sprinkling of beach huts offering some degree of privacy from the promenade above and we lay down together on the warm sand and scooped out our own little hollow. We embraced passionately and with increasing intensity. Marie gave herself to me willingly and without conditions, she was a very natural and loving person who obviously really enjoyed doing what came naturally. Marie was different to English girls in so far as she had no hang ups about religion, guilt about enjoying sex or fear of pregnancy. She sent me a postcard shortly after I returned to England but I heard nothing further after that. I wonder where she is now, probably a mid-fifties Boulogne housewife with six almost grown up kids.Oh youth, your lifespan is short like that of a butterfly, savour it while you can, you may never get the chance again.

Unfortunately, our stay in Boulogne came to an end and we moved to Le Touquet a pleasant seaside town popular with French and English alike. We were able to camp almost on the beach and in the next tent to ours was Morris a somewhat eccentric young Welshman with a terrific sense of humour. We had some very amusing days and nights out but unfortunately I didn't meet another Marie.

All good things come to an end and as our money was running out we started to contemplate our return. We packed up and headed back for Calais securing a lift most of the way in a pig van which stunk abominably and was driven by a maniac driver who nearly lost the plot when he skidded on a railway crossing and nearly hit a car. This time the white cliffs of Dover merely signified the start of the new school term. We managed to get lifts to the southern outskirts of London but had difficulty crossing the city as we had no money for public transport or even food. We started the long walk but it was very hot and after a couple of hours we stopped outside a small office block in central London feeling hot sweaty and tired. We sat on the pavement drinking copious amounts of water, feeling hungry but relieved to not have to shoulder the rucksack for a while.

A group of young female office workers were leaning out of a first floor window and asked us what we were doing. we briefly related our story, smiled and exchanged a few pleasantries and thought nothing of it. Just as we were about to leave one of the girls appeared on the pavement and gave us some money. They had felt sympathy for us and had organised a little collection. We moved off after offering our profuse thanks, bless you girls, it could not have come at a better time and restored our faith in human nature. As we moved down the road we bought bread and margarine with the money and lived off this for the next two days. We yomped across London with renewed vigour and by nightfall we had made the great north road. We had the good fortune to obtain a lift from a Scotsman returning to Edinburgh who wanted some company to keep him awake on the long night time drive north. He dropped us off in the middle of the night on the AI but only thirty miles from home. Another night was spent in a bus shelter awakening to another group of curious onlookers. One further lift and four hours of walking and we were home at last. What an adventure we had, I didn't stop eating for two days and it was bliss sleeping in a proper bed. My mother was very relieved to see me home as we had no home telephone and all she had received in two weeks was a postcard from Boulogne!

Drinking and the Sabbath

Sundays were without doubt the most boring days of the week requiring attendance at church scrubbed clean and dressed in the best clothes in order to endure a long service and equally long sermon. I was brought up as a Roman Catholic attending church at the very least every Sunday under threat of hell and eternal damnation if I missed a single day. The church, at the time, seemed to be naturally against anything remotely enjoyable or pleasurable. There was constant concern among the church leaders that parishioners may be using artificial methods of birth control when the

Pope's edict only allowed the rhythm method, known affectionately as Russian roulette, due to its impressive unreliability record. To defy the edict incurred a mortal sin meaning you couldn't take communion and would go to hell if you died before confessing the sin. In all this the immensely wealthy Vatican never had any regard for overpopulation, starvation or poverty. Personally I think it was all part of a cunning Vatican plan to keep the population under its thumb and sphere of influence.Lots of children often mean poverty, lack of educational opportunity and a perpetuation of the same lifestyle from generation to generation. Those who have a good education and the ability to question and challenge can make their own minds up and escape to better things.

Dancing too close to a non-spouse partner was considered potentially sinful and likely to lead to significant temptation! It always surprised me that priests and nuns, sworn to lifetime celibacy could be so knowledgeable on such matters and that the Pope could pronounce on them with apparent infallibility.

One of the first part time jobs I had was delivering Sunday papers which at least occupied Sunday mornings profitably. The whole round consisted of a barrow load of papers which took about three hours to deliver or a little less if assisted by my brother Ron. One of my fondest memories and highlights of the round was the need to avoid any number of fierce dogs lurking in customers' gardens. To be considered seriously poor in that section of society you had to have at least two fully grown Alsatian dogs the size of wolves for real street credibility.It was a great relief if the dogs were confined to the house but great care had to be taken when inserting the papers in the letterbox if all fingers were to be successfully retained. You could be sure that the brute lying in wait behind the door would still attempt to tear the paper to pieces before the owner got out of bed and attempted to restrain him. The tantalizing aroma of bacon and eggs wafting through the letterboxes would make me feel extremely hungry and more than ready for my own on return home. Thirst could be quenched en route by intercepting a milkman and downing a pint of milk in one attempt.

I also had a spell of grocery delivery using one of those heavy old black bikes with rod brakes, no gears and a large basket in the front. Progress was slow and somewhat unstable in windy conditions but journeys were short and the main trick was not drop anything. It was particularly annoying to drop something like a slab of butter which could not be beaten back into shape nor could the gravel be entirely removed from it which meant a return to the shop. Time between deliveries was spent stacking shelves and flirting in the stockroom with Betty and Christine, two sisters who worked in the shop and were a couple of years older than I. Unfortunately, a two-year age difference at the age is more like four as girls mature earlier and therefore there was little chance of dating them but at least we enjoyed the stockroom.

After church and work, particularly in the winter, there was little to do as all shops were closed and the religious fanatics made sure that they stayed so. Cinemas and other places of entertainment were also closed.Pubs however remained open and were well frequented particularly at lunchtime and also in the evenings although for some inexplicable reason they did not open until seven pm.

Drinkers and the Salvation Army were undoubtedly uneasy bedfellows but at the same time had a strange reliance on each other. The tradition of temperance was deeply rooted in mill towns but only in a minority of the populace, the majority being enthusiastic drinkers.Men were the beer drinkers and frequenters of pubs and women had a lot of catching up to do as the "ladette" syndrome was years away. Most women frequenting pubs without male escorts were perceived to be good time girls at best and glorified prostitutes at worst.Wine was considered an expensive delicacy for the upper echelons of society and beer the drink of choice for working men with the odd glass of whisky for special occasions.If you were a "real" man you smoked strong non filter brands such as Capstan full strength with the strong bearded sailor on the front of the pack. Apart from the women who frequented pubs very few smoked...

Most entertainment was arranged around local pubs within walking distance of home due to limited personal transport. Young men usually started drinking around the age of sixteen when they had outgrown the youth club and the challenge was to convince your landlord that you were really eighteen, the legal age to consume alcohol. It never ceases to amaze and puzzle me that young men can legally die for their country, smoke and have sex at sixteen but must be eighteen before they can legally enjoy a glass of beer. The strict licensing laws must be a throwback to Victorian times when there was ribald drinking and a pub on every street corner. The popularity of gin and the gin culture it spawned began to unravel society, particularly the women who often awoke from a drinking session with no recollection of where they had left the children. The influence of the prohibition movement hasn't helped in terms of reform but I suppose the only consolation is that you have to be twenty-one to drink in some American States.

The Working men's club is another particularly northern tradition, joining fees are low, beer is cheap and some of the profits are ploughed back into variety acts and cheap food. Originally almost entirely men only, women started to frequent and variety and dance nights were introduced.When I was a child you were only allowed to the door to look for your father and all that you could see through the smoke haze was a row of identically dressed flat capped men in line at the bar with pint glasses of beer in their hands. The flat cap is a strange tradition shared by the poorest workers and the aristocracy together.

The big night out for all was definitely Saturday as Sunday was the only day off most people had. Entertainment for young people was mostly in pubs once you had outgrown the youth club. The Saturday routine was to get into a pub around seven pm, down four or five pints and then get into the town hall dance around nine pm before the doorkeepers became too choosy and started denying access to suspected drunks. It was usually impossible to obtain alcohol in such an establishment but it was a happy hunting ground for all sorts of girls. There was a well-established and time honoured tradition that the girls stood by the wall on the right hand side of the dance floor and the boys by the wall on the left. The girls lined up displaying their attributes rather like cattle being inspected at the market and the boys looked at them from the other side of the floor and discussed the good ones with their mates. It took a brave man to cross that vast empty dance floor to ask a girl to dance and to risk the awful prospect of rejection and the long return across the floor with everyone watching. After a few false starts many boys and girls managed to get together although girls could be brutal in their rejections if you were too short, too young, didn't have the right clothes, hairstyle etc. Some girls who came every week never seemed to connect with anyone, despite approaches; maybe they were just too choosy. Just like today, no one seemed capable or able to judge beyond appearances.

One particular problem on a hot dance floor in those days was body odour, less common now due to the development of deodorants. I am sure men were equally to blame but I remember asking a beautiful girl to dance and she accepted. When we reached the dance floor and we started to dance

I gradually realised that she smelled like last week's gravy from the Sunday lunch and the problem then was how to gratefully disentangle myself.Bearing in mind the female embarrassment of bathing in a tin tub in front of the fire with several brothers all trying to have a crafty peep at the size of your breasts it's hardly surprising that bathing could be infrequent.

If you were lucky enough to escort the girl of your dreams home from the dance limited options were available. Virtually all girls lived at home until marriage in cramped and overcrowded conditions shared with a significant number of brothers and sisters. The best you could hope for would be a kiss and a cuddle down the side of the house, the more adventurous may try the garden shed or nearby fields and woods in the warmer weather.

I really do think that girls were sexier in those days than they are now, they also didn't expect perfection in a partner. In the days before the pill the excitement of a serious relationship was heightened by the ever present fear of pregnancy which girls would try to avoid but often their nature and biological make up would make them secretly wish for this to happen. For a girl from modest circumstances in a dead end job the thought of her own man and baby was an appealing prospect and given sexual ignorance and the lack of much choice in birth control many accidents did happen or were contrived. If you were in a serious relationship it was sometimes a fatal mistake not to take used condoms away with you as broody girls had been known to impregnate themselves after the event with certain proof of paternity and another poor guy hooked for life.

There was much more of a stigma attached to illegitimacy in those days and the majority of men caught out would do the decent thing and marry the girl. Social security payments and housing provision were far less generous in those days and so a single mother would struggle if she was kicked out of the family home. It also seemed far easier to establish a relationship in those days as no one was rich, no one wanted to be famous and virtually everyone was from the same social background.

But what to do if female company was uppermost in your mind and the pub and dance hall have failed. Why not try visiting family or older friends on Saturday nights when you know they are likely to be out.If their baby sitter doesn't have a boyfriend in tow she will probably be bored and only too willing to get to know you better.

Contraception in the form of condoms were usually obtained from men's hairdressers but it could be embarrassing purchasing these in front of a shop full of men awaiting haircuts all suddenly losing interest in the newspaper and giving you a knowing look.Chemist's shops were another source but inevitably you were served by a woman who would give you that naughty boy look or alternatively a lustful come on look which would have you reaching for the door knob, particularly if she was old enough to be your mother.The worse possible scenario happened to a friend of mine who went to the chemist and was sold the last packet on the display by the counter. Sharon, the insensitive shop assistant yelled out to her mate Maureen across the other side of the crowded store "Maureen have we got any more durex in the stockroom". The entire population of the shop looked round with renewed interest and vigour while my terminally embarrassed friend fled in panic through the door. No wonder mail order has grown in popularity

Irwin the Mad Marketer

On my return from France and the start of the new school term I needed to find a Saturday job and thought I would try the local market where a lot of casual work was available to those aged sixteen and over. I wandered around one morning making enquiries without any real success until I reached the bottom end of the market and Stamshaws large and busy fruit and vegetable stall.I was greeted in a no nonsense fashion by a man in his early twenties with a ruddy outdoor complexion and a shock of blonde curly hair. This was Irwin, the boss's son, who was quite a character in market circles as I was later to discover. He and I hit it off really well together from the outset and became firm friends.

Irwin had a great sense of humour and a unique robust quality about him; he lived life to the full on his own terms, did more or less whatever he wanted and didn't really care what others thought of him.He also made instant decisions, based on instinct, hired me on the spot, and told me to come to the warehouse at five thirty am the following Saturday to help load the lorries before setting up the market stall.Once the stall was set up I was to keep the stock topped up and eventually I would be let loose to serve the customers. The day would finish around six pm when the stall was dismantled, pay was one pound fifty pence a day plus all the fruit you could eat and heavily subsidized fruit and vegetables to take home to help the family effort.

The following Saturday dawned or rather I was up before the dawn when I arose at five am and cycled the three miles to Stamshaws warehouse which was situated to the rear, and on a lower level, than Stamshaws rambling old stone house. Mad Stan the lorry driver was already cursing the big lorry as part of his morning ritual.Originally from Barnsley he was some distant relative of the Stamshaws and had married a rather tarty looking bottle blond whom he always referred to as "arr lass" rather than refer to her real name which no one seemed to know anyway.

The Stamshaws biggest vehicle for the short journey to market was a large flat backed ex brewery lorry with a snub nose front. The headlights and radiator were configured in such a way that they always seemed to be grinning at you which was probably correct as the ugly brute would refuse to start most mornings. It was diesel powered but didn't have a choke and probably had missing or defective glow plug heaters. We usually ended up spraying an easy start aerosol into the engine air intake and if that didn't work five or six of us would push it in an attempt to bump start the beast.

Drama over we would arrive at the market and have about one and a half hours to assemble and stock the stall in time for our first customers at eighty thirty. If the lorry or stock from the wholesalers was delayed the timeslot became critical and would impact on the rest of the day. We would have the stall up and working within three hours of the start and it was then time for a well-earned breakfast. As the new boy it was my job to collect the chunky bacon sandwiches and pint mugs of steaming hot tea from a nearby refreshment stall. Irwin gave me the money and then said with great sincerity "By the way when you are there ask them for a bucket of the blue steam to wash the cauliflowers in". Thinking that this must be a fruit and vegetable trade secret treatment I went up to the stall and recited the order line by line. The Lady behind the counter took the order with a straight face and scuttled off into the back room. When she returned she said she had run out of blue steam but to tell Irwin they still had some yellow steam in stock if that was suitable. As I was the new boy and on my best behaviour I returned to the back of the stall, deposited the tea and sandwiches, and relayed the message about the steam whereupon everyone fell about laughing. Realising I had been taken for a ride I joined in and laughed at my own gullibility thereby ensuring my acceptance into the team.

Irwin and I were totally different in many ways but we always got on well together. I loved travel and couldn't wait to escape my grimy mill town to venture somewhere warm and exotic. Irwin was one of the last young men to have to endure National service in the army. This lasted all of two years all of which was spent in Germany and Irwin could not wait to return home at the end of his service. I was interested in education and self-improvement but Irwin could not see the point in it and was happy to return to his father's business.

Irwin had a younger brother Roger who was also a real character but not as sharp or businesslike as Irwin. He was about my age but generally kept away from the market business to run a couple of fruit and vegetable shops in nearby towns, much to Irwin's relief. The man in charge and head of the dynasty was Albert the father who was a flamboyant man who had successfully built up the business over the years. He was now semi-retired and his favourite pastime was horse racing and gambling on the results, sometimes very successfully, but not always. He ran a beautiful Jaguar car with walnut dashboard and leather upholstery which from the vantage point of my bike looked like some unattainable dream. I used to really enjoy the occasional ride in it if I was asked to help Albert with anything.

Irwin and I used to meet frequently in his local pub just across the road from his house. The Globe pub was a funny little place very small, just two rooms with outside toilets. Occasionally we would have a drink immediately after work but I preferred to go home and bathe and change first rather than sit around in dirty work clothes. Underage drinking was one of the main leisure activities, the only alternative being the cinema and Saturday night town hall dance. Irwin ran around town in a Triumph Herald Coupe, not state of the art but still a very nice car when I had just graduated to a moped and Dad ran a motorbike and sidecar. We used to venture out in it occasionally particularly on Sunday mornings to visit Pat, a young lad who used to work on the market stall with us until he was tragically paralysed in a rugby accident. Afterwards we would have a couple of lunchtime drinks and put the world to rights.

The people working on the market stall were an assortment of part time workers including some housewives and a few young girls. We would always ensure that our favourite young ladies were kept well stocked up with produce as it gave us the opportunity to chat them up at the same time. Working over twelve hours a day out in the fresh air in all weathers really made the cheeks glow and improved the appetite. The constant lifting and moving of boxes worked wonders for the muscle tone and general stamina. At the end of the day I would feel tired but the job worked wonders for my physique over the next two years.

As the months rolled by I achieved a position of considerable trust in the firm, safeguarding takings at the end of the day, taking money to the bank and so on. A night out with Irwin was always entertaining as he invariably had a joke or two to tell and an ability to consume vast quantities of beer. After a critical point in the beer consumption table, Irwin would begin to fancy himself as a matchmaker and as he seemed to know everyone in the pub, the choice was yours. However, if you were a little shy, like most young men, it could be very embarrassing. Irwin had been married and bitterly divorced, he had a girlfriend somewhere but he kept her to one side out of the business side of his life.

One night in the Globe he was feeling very mischievous and decided that a rather well built large breasted girl a couple years older than I was the girl of my dreams. From any angle Joan was a big girl with a mass of long black silky hair reaching almost to her waist, a tight red sweater emphasizing her ample charms and a tight leather skirt to complete the ensemble. Irwin engineered the seating arrangements when I was visiting the toilet so that when I returned I had no choice but to sit next to her and attempt to make some polite conversation. She was obviously flattered by the attention and seemed quite interested. I found out she lived just up the road and worked in a shop in town.

I was forced to spend the rest of the evening talking to her as Irwin studiously ignored me but very generously kept me well supplied with beer. After each new drink was consumed she somehow became more attractive and I am sure there must be a name for this syndrome which many other men must have experienced. After so much beer I felt the need to go to the toilet again and while I was away Irwin was telling her how much I liked her and how long I had had my eye on her but was too shy to act. By the end of the evening, when I was about to make a polite escape, she began to cling to my arm and become worryingly affectionate. Irwin, with impeccable timing, sealed my fate for the night by suggesting the area she lived in wasn't very safe and therefore as a young gentleman I should feel it my duty to escort her home.

Vowing to get my revenge I left the pub with Joan now in tow to the combined ribald comments of Irwin and his friends. We held hands and chatted on the ten-minute walk to her house but when we were close she dragged me down a dark alleyway for an amorous interlude. The evening's events seem to have stirred her loins for she was certainly hot and amorous. She grabbed me in a kind of female bear hug and rammed her tongue down my throat with the suction strength of an industrial vacuum cleaner. Once I had rediscovered a way to breath I thought what the hell and joined in the passion fueled by excessive alcohol consumption and my inability to break free from the bear hug, try as I may.

I slid my hands up her sweater to caress her back and scratch it gently and then I gradually moved my hands around her sides with thumbs outstretched to catch the first swell of her ample breasts. Her hips pushed forward to meet mine and we moved against each other in a kind of disjointed rhythm of desire. I was determined to see those lovely breasts, bigger than any I had seen before so I moved hands and thumbs around the front of her sweater and met with no resistance. After a while I became bolder and slowly lifted her bra to release those lovely orbs. Her bra was the size of David's sling as he prepared to do battle with Goliath but her breasts were surprisingly pert and upright as only young girls can be, two pendulous creamy orbs without blemish. I caressed them gently for a while and then turned my attention to her nipples, which in her excitement had grown to the size of small thimbles.I had to have a closer look at such beauty so I stuck my head under her sweater and inhaled deeply to absorb her unique scent as my head nestled between her breasts. I licked and teased her nipples with my tongue and rolled them very gently between my teeth.

Eventually I had to come up for air but Joan was still hot for love, she had told me she hadn't had a boyfriend for some time and it certainly felt like it. She started stroking my already excited manhood through my trousers. Many men are fascinated by leather skirts and I suppose I am no exception so I began concentrating on her generous thighs, gradually lifting her skirt in the hope of reaching teenage heaven. I ran my hands around the tops of her stockings and stroked that lovely piece of hot thigh remaining between the stocking top and the mound of Venus.

Joan's hands unzipped my trousers and one of them plunged in to seize my manhood roughly and with little finesse. I suspected she had little previous experience but at least she was willing and enthusiastic.I moved my hand slowly from her upper thigh and stroked her between her legs.

Her breathing quickened and I could feel she was soaking wet with latent desire. I slid my hand inside to caress her magnificent bush which was beautifully warm and very slippery and I slowly moved my fingers which slid easily into her tunnel of love.

Sadly, that's as far as it went in those days as the real fear of pregnancy, destitution and being cast out of the family home inevitably moderated behaviour. If a boy made a girl pregnant he was often expected to marry her regardless of their respective desires as this was considered the right thing to do. Joan and I decided to call it a night as it was one in the morning and her parents may be anxious she had not returned. I escorted her to her door, kissed her goodnight, and walked the four miles' home with a spring in my step. Joan had turned out to be a nice generous loving girl but sadly I never saw her again as I understand she moved to another town on a work transfer. I eventually got my revenge on the crafty Irwin by going to the fish market one day and obtaining some kipper scraps. I stuffed these down a piece of trim near the heater in his car to keep them warm and sure enough within a few days Irwin was moaning about the smell. I made the most of it by enquiring about his personal hygiene and asking if all his girlfriends smelled as good.

Eventually when he could stand it no longer I suggested that the car needed a full valet and that I would do it for three pounds on the basis that he only had to pay if I got rid of the smell. Easiest money I have ever earned!

Harry's Cars

Harry was a somewhat distant cousin who I hardly remember seeing at all when I was young but I got to know him very well I was around seventeen. He lived with his mother in an old stone house up a steep cobbled street in a forgotten backwater of town. Where once there had been mills and lots of houses now almost everything around Harry's house had been demolished leaving a weed strewn wasteland. The house was built on a hillside and I often used to stand in front of it trying to work out if the slope was steeper than I thought or if the house was leaning too. I could never work out why everything around the house had been demolished but Harry's house and one or two others in adjacent streets were allowed to remain, it was rather like being the few survivors from a catastrophic war, plague or natural disaster.

A big advantage of the house being built on a slope was that it had a magnificent cellar below. At one end there was good headroom and double doors to allow cars to be driven in and out. This facility enabled Harry to fulfil his dream and pursue the primary interest in his life to the total exclusion of anything else, other than the most persistent girls. He would pore over the local paper and advertisements for interesting old cars, buy whatever took his fancy and do them up in a fairly lethargic manner. He didn't really like the idea of selling them but occasionally did so to raise money for a new purchase.

Harry's real enjoyment was driving his collection, usually he didn't go far in his old bangers but a ten to twenty mile run on a nice sunny day was heaven to him. Unlike many collectors he didn't like the idea of such vehicles being hidden away in car museums and never used. To my young eyes his garage was a treasure trove of motoring memorabilia and as he was working full time he could afford to buy more cars than I had ever dreamed of.

The best old cars are undoubtedly convertibles and Harry shared the dream by buying mostly sports cars and his would change regularly as he bought and sold to finance his hobby. Often potential buyers would arrive to look at one car and drive off in another which had caught their eye. The lovely old upright MGs were one of my favourites. TCs TDs, and my personal favourite the slightly more modern and zippy TF. Harry had a slightly scruffy one in British Racing Green which went well and looked the part. On a nice sunny day there was nothing better than to climb aboard the TF with the hood down and potter around the town posing, admiring and smiling at the pretty girls as they did their shopping. The TF could have been mine for £100 but that was a lot of money in those days and I knew by then I would not stay long in the town of my birth. However, I still have indigestion when I see the prices they command today.

The other make of car which fired my imagination was the Morgan and in particular the Aero Morgan three wheeler which was a recent Harry acquisition and one of the most unusual cars I had ever seen. Again it was £100 bargain also in British Racing Green but there the similarity with any other car ended. The Morgan had two wheels at the front and one at the rear with a body the shape of an upturned bath tub. The engine was a massive V twin air cooled ex motorcycle unit bolted on to the front of the car just forward of the front wheels and displaying the J.A.P. logo of its manufacturer. Engine capacity was 1100cc and the car only weighed around 800 pounds therefore performance was brisk thanks to an excellent power to weight ratio.

We took the beast out on the road but in order to start it we had to operate the valve lifters, swing the massive starting handle vigorously and quickly let go of everything while the monster barked into life. If you held on you were likely to break a wrist. This Morgan didn't have any doors so to enter the driver stood on the seat and wriggled down into the cockpit past the steering wheel which had its bottom third cut away to facilitate entry. Foot controls were a footbrake and a cone clutch which was either in or out with nothing in between. Handbrake was outside and the accelerator was a lever on the steering wheel. Instrumentation was minimal but there was a rather intriguing oil pressure gauge which actually showed the oil flowing through it and had a knob which when turned increased or decreased the flow.

There was no hood which was just as well given the difficulties of entry. The top of the massive engine could be seen vibrating away at the end of the bonnet while the whole car shook and rattled like a motorbike. The chain driven rear wheel could be seen through a small hole in the wooden floor behind the front seats. There were no creature comforts such as heaters, seat adjustment, radio or hood in case it rained. Harry looked across at me, smiled and moved the hand throttle forward an inch whereupon the beast snarled and vibrated even more. We lurched forward as the primitive clutch took up the drive and the car shot off down the cobbled street the rock hard suspension and the three-wheel configuration finding every bump and groove in the road, very uncomfortable but great fun. We headed off into town on this Saturday afternoon in this unique creation which looked like a Tiger Moth aircraft with the wings sawn off. It certainly created lots of interest from the shopping fraternity, including several nubile young ladies, with its unique combination of looks and noise.

After a good run around the town and a few country lanes we parked up for a coffee remembering to park ready to exit as the beast had no reverse gear. Later when we returned to Harry's house we pushed it back into the garage to facilitate the next drive out.My hands smelled of engine oil and my teeth were still rattling with the vibrations as I made my farewells, jumped on to my motorbike and rode off into the night wondering if I could scrape up enough money to buy the thing.

Big Jim the Roofer

I first met big Jim when he sold me an old and somewhat decrepit motorbike in need of total loving care and attention for the princely sum of five pounds. It was an old BSA side valve of 250cc and I spent many a happy hour over the winter stripping it down in the cold garden shed.I needed somewhere warm to paint all the various bits and much to my mother's horror chose the spare bedroom which very soon looked like a motorcycle spares shop with bits hung up to dry all over the place.Spring arrived at last and I started the task of reassembly with a bit of help from my Dad.

In early April my pride and joy took to the roads resplendent in bright red, black and chrome giving me a new found freedom and mobility over the old Mobylette moped which I had purchased the year before also for five pounds. I had really enjoyed the restoration project and delighted in discovering the inner workings of the machine. I also knew how to fix it having rebuilt it!

Big Jim's house was in a stone terrace not far from my local pub. It was built on a slope and had cellars below which Jim used to house his motorbike collection. The place was veritable Aladdin's cave of motorcycling history. The rarest bike was an Aerial square four, a massive four-cylinder machine of 1000cc. When I sat on this monster my feet only touched the ground on one side but once I had kick-started the bike, the size, noise and power were awesome as I moved off with a bit of a wobble down the cobbled street.My favourite bike in Jim's collection was a racing Triton, a hybrid of Triumph engine in a Norton frame with sculpted dimpled fuel tank and beautiful alloy wheels with finned brake drums.

Jim was a roofer by trade and managed to secure me a summer job as a labourer in his team for the then substantial wage of twenty pounds per week, free of tax as I was a student. The first job we undertook was the re roofing of an old Victorian school in Huddersfield, three storeys high with high ceilings.Arriving on my trusty motorbike one day I was somewhat apprehensive about my new job and particularly working at heights I had never experienced before. The school had very high ceilings and the apex of the roof was at least sixty feet above the concrete playground. We started work, Jim bounded up this enormous ladder like a gazelle and sprung on to the roof climbing it diagonally using the laths for footholds with his arms slightly out at the side to balance himself. He signaled me to join him but by this stage my mouth was dry and my knees were knocking at the prospect. It all looked so easy but I knew it wasn't and I had no experience of heights. I decided I could not lose face in front of Jim so, not daring to look down, I took my first steps up the ladder gripping each side firmly with my hands and keeping my eyes firmly fixed on the sky. After what seemed an eternity I reached the top of the ladder and climbed onto the roof trying desperately not to look down. I balanced myself on the laths, trying to get used to the forty-five-degree angle of the roof, but had to grasp the laths with one hand so steady myself in the wind.

Jim gave his usual encouraging grin and I managed a not very confident smile in return. It was then I made the mistake of looking down, the ground seemed miles away, my legs felt like rubber and my mouth was so dry I could hardly speak.

Jim reassured me that I would soon get used to it but the thought of making that journey dozens of times a day with fifty pounds of tiles on my back filled me with horror. I survived the first day making little stacks of slates on the stripped roof at pre-arranged intervals so the roofers could work on undisturbed with a plentiful supply of raw materials. We had a short break in the morning and afternoon and lunch was normally sandwiches and a flask and occasionally fish and chips if there was a shop nearby. Work went on regardless of weather unless there was a torrential downpour but wet weather made the laths slippery and it was easy to lose footing and slide down the roof in such conditions desperately trying to grab anything to hold onto to stop the slide. The roofers worked on with single minded determination and oblivious to anything or anyone around them. On one occasion I watched a roofer tile a valley gutter working downwards with one knee on each slope until he ended up with a knee in each gutter. We had to shout at him to make him realise that one more step backwards and he would have landed in the children's playground.

Although roofing work was very tough it certainly built up muscles previously unknown and was not without its lighter moments. For instance, we discovered that if we arrived on site promptly at eight thirty, climbed the ladder to the roof and peered over the apex, we could see directly in to the bedroom of a pretty young lady who did her morning exercises topless in front of the open window at exactly the same time every morning.Confident she could not be seen from the ground she was oblivious to several pairs of eyes peering over the roof. The boss was also puzzled by this sudden and new found enthusiasm in terms of excellent timekeeping and prompt starts.

Much to my surprise Jim's prediction proved correct and after about a week I had gained greatly in confidence and balance on the roof. I could walk along the laths balancing with no hands and run up and down ladders without fear. However, one morning on the way to work my motorbike engine seized up and while I managed to ride out the resultant skid a half asleep scooter rider ran into the back of me. He ended up with a cut leg while I had a badly sprained ankle. I left the bike by the roadside and hobbled the two miles to work. This was a well-paid job which I did not wish to lose but the rest of the day was agony climbing ladders and working on the sloping roof., Later in the afternoon I had to attend the local police station to be interviewed after the accident. On arrival at the police station I found the attitude and line of questioning to be decidedly hostile and couldn't understand why as the accident had been caused by a mechanical failure and the scooter rider could have taken avoiding action if he had been paying proper attention to the road. Although I was only a young lad I refused to be browbeaten and remembered the scooter rider seemed to know the policeman at the scene of the accident. I decided to ask a few key questions particularly did any of the officers involved in my case know the other party prior to the accident or were they related in any way... I hit the jackpot as there was an embarrassed silence and much inspection of the ceiling.I then suggested that if this was the case I should be interviewed by another officer unconnected to either party. I also suggested, with a polite smile, that if I was to be charged with any offence I would seek an explanation from the Station Commander as to why I was interviewed without such relationship being declared. Needless to say no charges were forthcoming and I hobbled out of the station a few minutes later. In the meantime, Jim had kindly loaded my bike onto a pickup and taken it home arriving well before I did. Unfortunately, when my mother saw this out of the front window she had a minor fit thinking I must be hospitalised or something until Jim told her I was OK. I couldn't get hold of them earlier because for some inexplicable reason we did not have a domestic telephone. Dad kindly helped me to fix the bike and I was mobile again within two days.

We worked on a variety of buildings that fine summer getting sun tanned and fit in the process. By far the hardest job was re-roofing a farmhouse using stones like flagstones and often the same size, these weighed up to one hundred pounds each and had to be sized, cut and carried individually onto the roof.The strangest establishment we worked on was a large mental home just outside

Huddersfield, a grim forbidding looking Victorian building with a strange and varied collection of inmates. We were not supposed to fraternize with the inmates in any way but it was difficult to ignore people totally.One quite handsome lady was totally obsessed with tennis and would wander around begging people to have a game with her. On the basis of anything for quiet life the rest of the gang volunteered me to play with her as I was the only one willing to admit I had ever played the game. Although my participation made her day she was far too good an opponent for me and won every game and set.

We occasionally used to chat with the staff over a cup of tea. Their situation at work was almost as isolated as the inmates themselves and therefore they enjoyed meeting new people. Apparently most of the inmates free to roam were harmless and only the very violent and unstable had to be locked away. Both sexes were kept in the institution but strictly segregated with a high wire mesh fence dividing the recreation areas. However, nothing can stop the course of true love or true lust and one story in the institutional folklore is certainly worth recalling. It transpired that two inmates took a real liking to each other and would talk each other through the dividing fence for hours on end. Naturally the staff got a little bored with this day in and day out and eventually just ignored the two inmates who managed to take their affection to a new height through the chain link fence and the first institutional pregnancy resulted with red faces all around.

Going to the pub on Sundays was a great Yorkshire tradition but it did somewhat limit the rest of the day. Jim seemed to be always in attendance with many other friends and after several pints would often invite me home for Sunday lunch which was called dinner in the north. He lived with his mother who was a kind and generous woman who was always pleased to see me. Whatever roast dinner she was cooking she always made extra for the odd stray visitor with plenty of delicious gravy and Yorkshire pudding thrown in. After several pints and a roast dinner, the remainder of the afternoon passed in gentle lethargy either catnapping on the sofa or watching television.

Jim had a sister called Kathy who also lived in the house, she was quite tall and blonde and I had an on and off relationship with her for about a year. I think both Jim and his mother would like to have seen the relationship flourish but I knew where I was going and Kathy had difficulty in abandoning someone from a previous relationship. Thankfully Kathy was quite mixed up as she had an on and off relationship with a garage mechanic who Jim and his mother hated as he had been two timing her. It worked out very well in practice as every time Kathy got close to me this guy would get jealous and reappear to rekindle the relationship, thereby getting me off the hook and not upsetting Jim or his mother who would lay the blame at Kathy's door. Although we got on well most of the time and had a lot of fun together a serious relationship never really developed which was probably for the best as my time in Yorkshire was now quite short. A couple of weeks before my departure I went through the usual Sunday afternoon ritual of beer and dinner with Jim and family but we all knew this was coming to an end and I would miss these fine people. I sat on the sofa and began to ponder how my life would change immeasurably but Jim and his family would remain the same.

In my new life I could already sense friends, outlook and dress would all be different and I would travel the world experiencing things that many people could only dream about it. It is always difficult leaving the people and places you know but it has to be done, I wonder if Kathy ever married her mechanic?

Escape to a New Life

Imagine the restlessness of youth bursting with adventure and enthusiasm, impatient to see and make his mark on the world, yes this was I at the age of eighteen. Instead of enjoying and experiencing these things I was cooped up in a sixth form classroom bored rigid by pure math's and looking out over the school playing fields dreaming of what may be over the next hill or rise.

Of course a University education was the goal of many but why? I could have gone to University to read engineering but despite my interest in things mechanical this did not appeal. I needed something with a bit more excitement to it and had no real desire to end up as an underpaid boffin undervalued by society in a way only England can treat engineers and technical people. My dilemma and distractions were greatly magnified by my healthy appreciation of the female form and as there were several girls in the class this proved to be an easy preference when compared to the delights of pure maths.

An idea began to form in my head that I may like to experience life in the Navy, lots of travel and some adventure plus excitement in return for discipline and some boring routines. My father had joined the Navy on the outbreak of war as an able seaman and always had lots of tales to tell in true boys own style, having travelled the world and thankfully, but only just, survived. The Navy seemed to have given him discipline, confidence, a sense of humour, comradeship and excitement particularly in comparison with his post war routine life in the chemical industries. He landed troops on the shores of Anzio, Sicily and many other beachheads experiencing many horrors in the process. After successful landings and advance from the beachheads in Anzio he decided not to remain with his landing craft on the beach and slept in a ruined building instead. Early the following morning the craft was hit by a dive bomber and little remained but the authorities found a few possessions marked "RT RC" which was my father's initials and his religion, Roman Catholic.

The telegram winged its way home with the inevitability of war, each street looking out for them and wondering who could receive it this time. It duly arrived at his father's house stating he was missing, believed killed in action. Meanwhile back in Anzio Dad returned to what was left of his landing craft and realised he had made the right decision the night before. In the chaos of the landing he was never informed of the telegram and the authorities somehow did not react to his survival. Several weeks later a happy smiling Dad arrived home and knocked on the door and marched in. He was met with screams and stares of fright and disbelief, they thought he was a ghost.

Perhaps in view of his Dad was less keen than I thought

he would be about my plans but nevertheless realised that I had to make my own life and my own decisions. There was also a certain amount of disbelief that I was applying for direct officer entry when I came from a humble working class background.At that time the officer training school at Dartmouth was dominated by public school entrants many of whom had been specially groomed for service life at military style public fee paying schools such as Pangbourne. My mother I know had her own strong reservations based upon the emotional turmoil she had been through with Dad but by and large she kept her own council and just worried quietly.

I raised the subject with my headmaster, a Rosminian priest, at a careers session. His comments were "surely you can find a more honourable profession" From his very narrow viewpoint only the church, teaching and universities were worthwhile professions. He did however show a remarkable ignorance of certain parts of English history when I reminded him that in my own very small way I was following the call of Admiral Lord Nelson, one of England's greatest heroes, and that kept him quiet.

I did have my longer term revenge however by tipping off the Royal Navy recruiting office that there was a great untapped source of recruits at the school and very little information on careers in the military available. The result was that over the next few years the school was bombarded by military displays and careers advisor and while I was the first to join the navy I was certainly not the last.

At first I did not think that I had much chance of Officer selection given my background and lack of knowledge of service life but I was invited down to HMS Sultan in Lee on Solent for a three-day assessment covering a variety of tasks and tests to determine my suitability or otherwise. Initially this all seemed a little daunting particularly the Admiralty Interview Board who, with the exception of a couple of civilians, were all Senior Naval officers in their finest with more: "scrambled egg" on their caps than I had ever seen before. The first test was a practical one in the gym, how to get a mine over a hypothetical river and safely to the opposite bank without blowing it and the team up. I was pleased to see that this was all good Boy Scout stuff, much of which I had experienced before involving ropes, beams and assorted block and tackle. This was good fun and so absorbing I forgot the assessment board were even present.

The next task, in total contrast to the first involved surviving a one to one interview with a psychiatrist a very strange person whose opening line was "do you still wet the bed". Having dealt with that one we moved on to discuss a number of other topics such as relationships with parents, underage drinking, growing up and promiscuity. He really was a strange person but not too difficult to deal with in the thrust and parry of debate. I hoped he was looking for a balanced person who could debate topics and be assertive when required but did not exhibit any extreme characteristics. A number of other tests and assessments took place over the next two days and I finally commenced the long journey home tired out but reasonably happy with my performance and just a slight tinge of optimism.

A couple of weeks passed by and one morning over breakfast a large envelope winged its way through the letterbox and landed with a thud on the mat. I knew exactly what it was and with butterflies in my stomach I picked it up and started to open it with trembling hands. I started to read the letter but my anxious eyes skipped down to the middle of the page and picked out the important words I HAD BEEN ACCEPTED for officer training subject only to a medical. I was to train to be a seaman officer for bridge watch keeping, gunnery and navigation duties. My feet didn't touch the ground for the rest of the day particularly as I knew that only thirty-five percent of candidates invited for interview actually got through. However, the really sobering thought was that only forty percent of those accepted for training would survive the first year and pass out of the Naval College to join the fleet.

The medical was very nearly my undoing when it came to correctly identifying the colour of a pin point of light representing the port or starboard bow light of distant ship. The staff seemed to be in a bit of a hurry and took me from a well-lit to a darkened room and commenced the test immediately. I knew this procedure was incorrect as even the best eyes require time to adjust from bright light to darkness and therefore I would not perform as well as I should in this test. This proved to be the case so I politely demanded a recount explaining why.In the circumstances they were obliged to agree and I passed. This sloppy initial procedure could have finished my career before it started and I learned there and then to always have the courage of your convictions whether it makes you popular or not.

At last the day of departure drew near and I began, quite naturally, to become apprehensive and have mixed feelings about leaving but at the same time nothing was going to stop me and I was determined to succeed. I had enjoyed a happy childhood in a close and loving family, we never had much money but we had a lot of fun. I was to appreciate this even more when I made friends with boys from more affluent backgrounds who had been deposited into the public school system aged nine and left devoid of parental love and contact.I knew I would be homesick for a while as the Britannia Royal Naval College was at the opposite end of the country from home and a long way to travel in those days. This was however the adventure I had yearned for. While my school friends were going off to teacher training college or taking jobs locally, marrying young and having similar lifestyles to parents I would be doing something completely different.

The transition from youth to man, the escape from often dreary mill town life to a real career was mine for the taking, all I had to do was make it work.

At last the morning of departure arrived. I was the eldest child and the first to leave home, smartly dressed, haircut and bags packed. Dad shook my hand and wished me well in a manly but slightly dewy eyed way. Mother was weeping uncontrollably as only mothers can, clutching her pinafore and thinking I may never return as Dad nearly had. The wrench of departure is always sad but inevitable. Out of the door, into the taxi. Last farewells, look straight ahead and think positive. It's lovely September morning, the sun is shining, I'm going on a long journey to start my first career and bring fulfilment to my restless and adventurous spirit. What is more important I am no longer a boy but a man who is about to see what is over the next hill and the one after that.

So what happened in my new life? well I had all sorts of adventures and escapades but that's another story for another day.

www.ingramcontent.com/pod-product-compliance
Lightning Source LLC
Chambersburg PA
CBHW071945190726

48293CB00004B/1347